A KISS STOLEN

GEORGIA LE CARRE

ACKNOWLEDGMENTS

Many, many thanks for all your hard work and help,
Caryl Milton
Elizabeth Burns
Nichola Rhead
Teresa Banschbach
Tracy Gray
Brittany Urbaniak

A Kiss Stolen

ISBN 978-1-910575-87-1

PROLOGUE

Jake
https://www.youtube.com/watch?v=6c1BThu95d8
(She's a Rainbow)

"*D*ad, I'm moving out."

I stare at my daughter in astonishment. "What? Why?"

She straightens her shoulder and her jaw takes on that intractable line it does when she's absolutely determined to do something come hell or high water. "Because," she says firmly, "I'm going to be twenty in a few days and it's about time."

I frown. "Why is it about time?"

"Dad," she cries exasperated. "All my friends moved out of their parents' houses like two hundred years ago."

I fold my arms. "That's not a reason."

She folds her arms with equal determination. "Come on, Dad, be reasonable. I want to move out because I want my own space."

"You have your own space here. Hell, you have a whole wing to yourself. No one ever bothers you there ... not since you put excrement in your brother's bed for coming into your space, anyway."

"For heaven's sake, stop bringing that up. I was nine years old when I did that," she says crossly.

"My point remains. Nobody ever disturbs you in your part of the house."

She uncrosses her arms and leans forward, her bright blue eyes shining. "No, Dad, I mean, I want to be independent. I want to have my own little apartment in London. I want to paint the walls myself in the color I choose. I want to wake up in the morning and nip down to the bakery for some croissants or an apricot Danish that is still hot from the oven. I want to open my window and look down on a busy street full of people rushing to work. At night, I want to lie in my bed and to listen to the sounds of people coming back from pubs and clubs. I want the electricity bill to have my name on it. And when the postman rings I know the package is for me. I don't want a big place. Just a one bedroom apartment or a studio would do me fine. Actually, if I had a choice I want a tiny cramped place so I can make it really cozy. Something like the movie version of the apartment Bridget Jones was living in."

I sigh. I came from nothing and my dream was to live on the biggest house in the street. My daughter has lived in absolute luxury all her life and now her big dream is to go live the life of a poor person in London. How could I fight the romantic draw of poverty?

"Please, Dad."

I hate the idea of her leaving home. It doesn't feel right. It's been a long time since I've had such a strong instinct warning me against something. My instinct never failed me before.

"You didn't expect me to commute every day to London to finish my Internship in the city, did you?" she asks incredulously.

"Yes, as a matter of fact, I did. It is barely an hour's drive and I've already arranged for your transport."

"No, that's not what I want. Please, Dad," she pleads. "I can't live at home forever. Anyway, I'll come home for the weekends."

I look at her and realize suddenly, as if it crept up on me without warning, that my little girl has grown up. Not only has she grown up, she wants to spread her wings and fly away. For years I refused to allow myself to think of this day, but it is here now and I can't control it. I see her as a stranger. An incredibly beautiful woman, with long black hair, and sparkling sapphire eyes. It makes me afraid. I choose my words very carefully. "All right—"

She jumps out of her chair, starts whooping and doing a Red Indian dance.

"I'm not finished, Liliana," I say.

She stops and looks at me suspiciously.

"You can move out, but you must stay at our apartment in London."

Her face falls.

"Nobody," I continue, "from our family will come unless you invite us. It will be yours only. You will have complete privacy."

She slumps back into the chair and exhales loudly. "Dad, you don't get it, do you? I don't want to live in a grand four-bedroom apartment in the middle of Mayfair with a live-in chef and a cleaner coming in five times a week. I want my own little place with a tiny kitchenette where I will cook my own meals and maybe I will throw a small dinner party where everyone has to sit on cushions on the floor. I want to be completely independent."

"Fine, fine. Just give me a few months and I will buy a smaller apartment for you outside Mayfair. Perhaps Knightsbridge or Kensington?"

She stands up. "Dad, the truth is you didn't let me finish. I don't need you to find me an apartment because I've already found the perfect little place in Victoria. It's above a cute little hairdresser for boys. The chairs where the kids sit look like little cars." She chews her bottom lip. "I've also already paid the deposit. I'm moving in next week."

Now, it's my turn to slump into my chair.

"I'm sorry, Dad. I know it's hard for you, but I'll come back every weekend. I promise, it'll be like I never left at all."

I search her eyes. "What about your mother? Have you thought how this will affect her?"

Her voice is gentle. As if she is the adult and I am the child. "I told her last night and she was okay with it."

I frown. How strange. Lily never said anything. She was

normal. Then I remember she held me tightly when we got into bed and said the strangest thing. "You will stay with me until the very end, won't you?" I kissed her and when I looked into her eyes she seemed vulnerable and lost. And it made me remember that incomprehensible time she miscarried. It makes the hairs on my neck stand to think of that period. How she became a total stranger. Even now it hurts to think she wanted to die. She actually contemplated leaving us all.

My daughter moves quickly and crouches at my feet. She takes both my hands in her delicate soft ones. "I haven't forgotten, Dad," she whispers.

I look into her eyes and nod. The memories swim in my head. I see my daughter again as a seven-year-old child lying next to my wife in our bed. The curtains are drawn shut. "Mummy," she asks in a pitiful voice. "Are you angry with me? Have I done something wrong?" And my wife says nothing. Silent tears pour from her open blank eyes. I rush into the room and pick up my confused, frightened child from the bed. Her cheeks are wet. I hold her close to my body. "You've done nothing wrong, my darling. Nothing. Mummy is just not very well." And my wife lies there in the semi-dark, unmoving, unresponsive, trapped in her black world of unrelenting sorrow.

I don't realize that my own cheeks are wet until Liliana wipes them with her thumbs. "She'll be all right. That time is past now. You'll see. As long as she has you, she'll be all right."

I nod. "She'll always have me."

CHAPTER ONE

Liliana

$\mathcal{I}$ huddle into my favorite Firebee jacket as Moose, my pet dachshund, and I make our way over to the French bakery around the corner. Moose is urging me along enthusiastically. His stubby legs moving quickly and his golden-brown fur fluttering in the cold wind.

I notice with some alarm that his butt seems a lot rounder. Can it be that he has put on all this extra weight since we moved here a week ago? I must be feeding him too much, or the wrong things. I'll have to check with Mum. It has been mostly her job feeding him.

"Oh, dear, you're getting a bit thick around the middle too, Moose," I mutter more to myself than anyone else, but almost as if he'd heard me, my sensitive hotdog of a pet suddenly stops walking, and looks up at me reproachfully.

My pause is equally as abrupt. The smile drains from my face at his accusing gaze. "I was only joking. You know I'd never fat shame you. You're a hottie not a fattie."

With a look of utter disgust, he continues on his regal way.

Holly, the owner's daughter, is behind the till at the Patisserie. She has freckles sprinkled all over her nose and cheeks and unruly red curls that refuse to be contained or restricted by the white cap she is wearing. Her face breaks into a wide grin. "Cold enough to freeze a monkey's balls out there, isn't it?"

I laugh at her colorful description. While Moose greedily wolfs down the biscuit she gives him and her cheerful chatter washes over me as I cast my eyes over all the goodies inside the glass counters. A pretty little pear tart with icing sugar dusted all over it catches my eye.

Holly puts it into a pink box, ties a blue ribbon around the box, and I pay for my purchase. Outside the pavement is already full of people hurrying to work. I stop and take a deep breath of the freezing morning air and can't help feeling that my life is like a wonderful dream. Sometimes at night I have to pinch myself because I can hardly believe how lucky I am.

As we retrace our steps back to my apartment it is a job avoiding Moose's unsubtle glances. From me to my box then back to me, then back to the box. I know he is trying to force me into a silent promise to share my treat. I resist for most of the journey, but eventually give in when we arrive at the entrance to my apartment building and he starts leaping and circling so excitedly around me, it's near impossible to handle his leash. "Okay, okay, I'll give you some," I capitulate.

He immediately stops jumping and sits down in the foyer in anticipation. I gather the thick warm bundle of flesh up into my arms and he licks my face happily in the elevator.

≈

*A*n hour later, the pear tart is history, and I am dressed in a newly ironed soft pink shirt and my navy suit. Standing in front of the floor length mirror in my bedroom I look critically at my reflection. My long black hair is neatly held back with clips. My face is carefully, but lightly made up free of all make-up, but a touch of lip gloss.

Today I will check off another first in my life.

The first day of my internship at Osborne & Nesbit. I'd sent in my application like every other eager applicant salivating for a taste of the industry. Their response came too suspiciously fast and I guessed it was either my surname had once again opened doors that are usually tightly shut for any normal dreamer, or my father had taken it upon himself once more to meddle in my life.

It used to irritate me a lot that I couldn't beat my own path, but a long time ago I learned to give thanks for my good fortune. I swore to myself I would prove I was something more than just a billionaire's spoilt kid.

Moose sees me to the door and after lots of noisy kisses I am on my way to the elevator. As it descends my phone begins to vibrate inside my briefcase. I pull it out and click accept.

"Hey, Mum."

"Have you already left for work?"

"Yup, I'm in the elevator."

"Look, honey. Dad had business in London and he's literally five minutes away from you. Wouldn't it be easier for him to pick you up and take you to work?"

I sigh. "Mum, when was the last time Dad had business in

London that necessitated him driving here at this time of the morning?"

Mum says nothing.

"Exactly. Mum, you and Dad have to let me get on with it. I want to take the tube to work. I want to be like all the other interns. I don't want to arrive in a Rolls Royce."

"Dad didn't take his Rolls. He knew that would embarrass you. He's in his Mercedes."

I push down the small niggle of frustration that tries to take hold in my brain. "Mum, you understand how I feel, don't you? I want to be independent and make it under my own steam."

"I guess so," she says softly. "But it's just that Dad and I are worried about you. You're so young and London is a dangerous place for an innocent girl. We have protected you all your life so you won't even see danger coming. You—"

"Jesus, Mum, anyone would think I was some sort of spy being sent into the dangerous underbelly of the criminal world. It's broad daylight outside and I'm going to work at a lawyers' firm! Everything is going to be just fine."

"All right." Her voice is heavy. "Are you still coming back home this weekend?"

"Of course."

"Good." She sounds so happy I feel bad I got irritated with her a moment ago. I know how delicate she is. I have never forgotten how she slipped into such a deep depression it was months before Dad could bring her out of it.

"Mum?"

"Yes, honey."

"Why don't you come over tomorrow and have lunch with me? We could meet at one of the restaurants near work and we cou—"

"Oh yes, that is such a brilliant idea," she cries eagerly.

"Okay, I'll call you tonight, and tell you the name of the restaurant."

"Have a good day at work, darling. I know you will be amazing."

"Thanks, Mum. I love you."

"I love you too. With all my heart."

"Bye, Mum," I say happily, as I run down the steps of my building and onto the busy street full of people rushing to work. This independence is what I crave, I think, as I join the rest of the city's workers on their way to corporate enslavement.

CHAPTER TWO

Liliana

My first day is a whirlwind of activities and people, but it eventually winds down to an after-work drinks session at the Marquis of Granby, an 18th century dark-wood pub, around the corner from our offices.

I perch on a bar stool with one of my fellow interns, Francine, and stare moodily into my drink. Yes, I found out pretty quickly my father's net worth is no secret along the hallowed corridors of Osborne & Nesbit. More people than I would have liked treated me as if they were terrified to piss Jake Eden's daughter off.

"Stop looking miserable," Francine says as she calls out to the waiter. "You'll make the rest of us hate you even more."

I lift my head and look at her. She is the opposite of me, with cherry red lips and masses of blonde hair. I brush my hair away from my neck with a sigh. "I am not miserable. Aggravated would be a better term."

"I only have one question," she says and swivels to face me. "Did you apply for the internship yourself?"

"What do you think? My dad's secretary did? I applied to all twenty companies myself."

Her beautiful brows furrow in surprise for a moment. "Why?"

"Because I didn't realize how many people wanted to kiss my father's ass and I'd heard it would be incredibly hard to get a place."

She laughs. "It is. So your only crime is having a father with too much money?"

"For now," I respond.

"Why? Are you thinking of adding more titles?"

"Maybe. I might have to become overbearingly rude to the men who pretend to like me simply because they want to get to know my father," I say thinking of Steven, another fellow intern, and his obsequious behavior at lunch. He was genuflecting so much his nose was almost in his soup.

Francine receives our drinks and pushes mine towards me with a wink. I take an immediate sip.

"Yes, I saw what the fool Steven was doing, but it's too late to pull off that title, I already like you. A lot. I mean, really a lot."

I glance sideways at her. "Hmmm ... is that your attempt at impressing me?"

She cowers comically, back slouched, tone sheepish, eyes shifty. "Is it working? I really need a full-time gig here after this internship is over."

She looks so funny I can't hold my laughter back. Maybe this internship is going to be all right, after all.

She takes a sip of her drink. "The buttering up aside, do you have your eyes on any of the guys from our team?"

"Nah. Do you?"

Her head tilts slightly towards the tall French intern in our party. I noticed earlier that he has been turning both female and male heads alike. "He's so goddamn full of himself," she spits. "I'm obsessed."

I eye the green-eyed, dark-haired, calve-length coat clad stud. "He's very handsome, but way too obvious for me."

"Obvious? What's wrong with that?" she asks indignantly before turning to gaze dreamily in his direction. "He looks like fun. If I don't get a full-time position here at the end of the day, he'll be mine … at least for one night."

I smile. "You don't spit into your own rice bowl?"

"Never." She turns back to me. Her eyes are sparking with a need for drama. "But you … you have a story to tell, and I want to hear it."

I raise an eyebrow. "Story?"

"You're carrying a torch for someone, aren't you?"

My eyes widen. No way she can tell. "What makes you say that?"

"I don't know, but I can always tell when someone's "I'm available" light is off and it's always because their heart's taken."

I bite my lip. Never in my life has anyone asked about him. He is my deepest secret and regret. I have never forgotten him and never stopped wishing I had never told Dad about him. Over the years it has become a recurring dream. In my dream, he is not the boy who kissed me, but a beast. An angry, revengeful beast. I have never spoken about him to anyone. Not even Mum or my best friend and it feels very good that someone else has recognized something so important to me.

"Spit it out," Francine urges impatiently.

I take a deep breath. "It's a pathetic story, and not very adult like either."

She grins. "Now I'm even more intrigued."

"You'll probably laugh, but here goes. For some weird reason, I kept the son of our gardener in my heart for long time. Well since I was eleven."

"The gardener's son? I need snacks for this," she says, "and a refill." She places her order, and immediately turns to look at me expectantly. "Go on. Was he raking you instead of the leaves?"

"No, he wasn't. There's actually not much to the story. It was just one stupid episode."

"One episode? Wow, what happened?" she asks, popping a salted cashew nut into her mouth.

"Well, he grabbed me and kissed me. I was so young I didn't understand how fragile his situation was. I ran back to the house and told my dad. He kicked both him and his father out. End of story. I haven't seen either of them since."

She looks vaguely disappointed. "So no one was thrown in jail?"

I shook my head.

"So why is he still on your mind? Wait, how old was he?"

"Fifteen."

"Hmm. Does that mean you haven't dated anyone since then?"

I pick out a Wasabi covered peanut from her bag. "Honestly?"

"Of course." She grins. "We are training to be lawyers here."

"No."

"Shit," she whispers. "Must have been a damn good kiss."

"It was ... primitive, but I didn't sleep for days after."

"Whoa! I wish someone would give me a primitive kiss."

I shrug. "It's probably not the kiss. Just one of those unre-solved issues in your life that messes with your head and—"

"Incoming," she interrupts.

At the warning I turn my head and sight Steven coming my way.

"Are you in the mood to have your ass licked?"

"Ugh. The things you say." I slide off my stool. "I'll be in the Ladies."

"I'll get rid of him in five."

On my way to the Ladies I start to regret telling Francine about the gardener's son. I don't even know why I told her. She's practically a stranger. Worse, it's probably changed the way she sees me. Even I can see how pathetic and senseless it is to allow that ancient incident to hold such a momentous importance in my life, but I can't help it.

I simply can't let go.

All the cubicles are empty and I stand alone in front of the mirror and stare into my own eyes. They are cloudy. As usual any thoughts of him automatically weigh down on my spirit. It is almost like a loss I can't get over. The way my mother still grieves for her lost baby. I have even seriously considered looking for him and apologizing. Maybe that will free me and make me see that the memory of him as the tortured, tragic, dark-eyed savage and his grand passion is something my young, impressionable brain has idealized out of all proportion.

For all I know he may have become absolute scum or a terrifying sociopath.

Maybe then the memory of the first time my heart fluttered will no longer be an open wound, but simply a faint scar. Maybe then I will stop devouring every second-chance romance I can lay my hands on. The rational part of me knows these books are just a fantasy, but the irrational part of me doesn't care. It wants what it wants. I've drowned myself in fantasy after fantasy of such tales. They are sweeter to latch onto than the sad reality of a boy I cannot get out of my mind after all these years.

"Excuse me."

My heart jumps at the interruption and my head whirls around. At first I am not sure why I feel so bothered at the presence of the man standing just inside the door. He is clad in a blue and white checkered dress shirt and a pair of dark jeans. His face is weathered, his hair a dirty blond, and his eyes a lifeless blue.

Then I realize why my body instinctively contracted with fear. I am standing in front of the sink of the women's bathroom. I force a smile to my lips. "This is the women's bathroom," I point out, in the wild hope that for some unfathomable reason he truly does not realize so.

His watery blue gaze doesn't waver. It remains steadily on mine. He doesn't even blink, and I know then that I am in deep trouble. Unable to hold his dead gaze I lower my eyes, turn on the faucet, and pretend to wash my hands while my panic-stricken mind tries desperately to remember what my father taught me to do, but the only thing I can remember is my father telling me to be vigilant at all times. A bit late for that though.

"I need to know what the time is, please?"

"I'm not wearing a watch," I say as casually as I can, and lifting my eyes I look directly at his reflection. I need to keep him talking. Someone is bound to come in.

"That's a shame," he murmurs, taking a step forward.

Oh God, my dad's greatest fear is going to be realized. I am going to be kidnapped! My pepper spray is in my purse, but my purse is zipped up. I try not to show the panic clawing at my heart. I remember Dad saying, *Scream. Scream as hard as you can.* I open my mouth to yell, but in an instant, he is on me.

A callused hand wraps around my mouth and the thick pungent smell of sardines and onions overwhelms me just as I feel a sharp prick on my upper arm. I continue to struggle with all my strength, but I sense my limbs becoming heavy. My vigorously beating heart seems to slow down, and all I can think about is my father. He is going to be royally pissed, and I am now most definitely never going to be free from his surveillance, perhaps for the rest of my life.

CHAPTER THREE

Liliana

I awake in a pitch-black room not knowing who I am, or where, or how long I have been here.

Then the fog in my brain lifts and I remember. Instantly, a deep fear overtakes me, to the point I cannot move at all. I dare not even breathe. Shutting my eyes, I think of my father. I see his strong face. What would he do if he were in my shoes? He would *never* lay down and die. He would fight until his dying breath. I open my eyes and try to make sense of my surroundings. I am not in some garage shed somewhere in the middle of nowhere.

I realize I am fully dressed in my own clothes. My body has no pain and I'm lying on clean smelling sheets, the mattress is extremely comfortable. I am also not bound in any way. My frightened brain finds the least threatening explanation: I've been itching to get out from under my father's wings to chart my own way, but to him I'm just ripe to be scammed, cheated and abused, so this is a trick he's pulling on me to teach me to be more vigilant.

Slowly, careful not to make any sound in case there is someone else or thing in the room with me, I sit up. When my bare feet hit the ground, they connect with the roughness of a cheap rug. I stand with my hands stretched out in front of me and carefully grope my way in the dark to the nearest wall. Then I begin to feel for a door. My hand closes over a handle. Hardly daring to breathe I turn it. It is firmly locked, of course. I exhale slowly.

Hopefully, the light switch will be right by it.

In a few seconds, I find it, and feel the tears of relief rush to my eyes. Drawing in a quick breath and saying a little prayer, I flip the switch. A naked lightbulb in the middle of the room bursts into harsh light. My eyes hurt with the sudden glare, and I squeeze them shut before squinting into the brightness.

I am in a medium-sized room, bare but for a bed and a cupboard. The walls are freshly painted in magnolia and the floor is grey concrete. The idea that it could be my own father doing this to teach me a lesson in vigilance dissipates instantly. Dad would rather cut off his own hand than imprison me in a drab room like this, and even if he did, Mum would never let him.

I look around, more confused than ever. It must be the effect of the drug the man had used to knock me out earlier, but my thoughts feel slow and disconnected. I find myself going towards my shoes, slipping them on and heading to the only window in the room.

I pull the green drapes apart. A metal barricade surrounds the window. Looking beyond I can see absolutely nothing but a thin slice of moon in the sky, a few dots of lights from the stars, and the velvety dark silhouette of trees. I gaze down at my empty wrist and regret not putting on a watch. If

I had to guess the time I'd put it to be the early hours of the morning.

I need a plan.

I wonder if banging on the door and demanding an audience with whomever has orchestrated this nightmare is the right way to go. I turn around then, and that is when I see it: the dark lens staring down at me. The entire room, I am sure, is in its view. My hands begin to tremble. Not with fear but fury. I walk towards the surveillance camera.

"Why am I here?" I demand.

Silence.

"I'm awake now. There's no need to waste either of our time so just state what you want and we can end this stupid charade."

Silence.

"Is it money? If it is the sooner you get down here the sooner we can stop this charade and the money hits your bank account."

Silence.

Furious, but not stupid enough to tick anyone off with the barrage of insults that wants to burst from my mouth, I turn around and head back to the bed. I take a seat and stare directly into the camera.

"I'm waiting," I say, and that is exactly what I do.

The time ticks by, and a strange grogginess, probably a lingering effect of the drug administered earlier begins to take effect again. My eyelids begin to feel as heavy as lead, and my head starts to nod, but with a jerk I straighten up and stare ahead. Time passes before I hear footsteps outside the door. I instantly jump to my feet, then check myself and sit back down. The handle of the door is pulled down.

I am terrified, but I curl my hands into fists, harden my gaze, and stare at the door. It opens and a man fills in the doorway.

He is a *ten*.

This is all my muddled, terrified brain can muster up. My jaw drops and I stare at him in confusion. His shoulders are broad, his hair is raven-black, and he is dressed from head to toe in black, but what sends a chill through me are his eyes. They are like tar-slicks. Shiny and utterly opaque. There is no doubt he is dangerous, and the way he looks at me ...

I spring to my feet in an instant.

He stands very still and regards me from beneath his sooty lashes. Like a wild animal watching its prey, and for a moment I am sure I am going to be raped.

"Who are you?" I ask, but even as I ask that question something else clicks in my brain. He looks familiar. His face, the oval way it is structured and those eyes ... the chill I experienced had been from a trigger of familiarity, not fear. My facade of coolness snaps and an angry yell erupts from my throat. "Who the fuck are you?"

His response is an amused snicker, and my heart nearly stops.

CHAPTER FOUR

Brand

https://www.youtube.com/watch?v=qrO4YZeyloI

*M*y, my, but little Liliana Eden has grown up to be one fiery woman. A fucking gorgeous one too. Her hair is long and thick, her nose is small and neat like her mother's, and her eyes are as haunting as I remember. Her lips, however, are still my favorite feature. To put it simply they are audaciously plump, the top one almost overlapping the lower and giving her the look of a sulky whore. With a mouth like that all you have to do is pout your lips and the whole world would do your bidding.

I desperately want to slip my tongue into that bitchy mouth: to see if she still tastes the same. Of bubblegum. She will bite down and injure me, but the thought only rocks my cock. My gaze drops down to the full chest straining against the soft pink blouse. It makes my hands itch. The fleshy mounds are begging to be fondled and sucked. I can already see myself dragging my tongue down to her tiny waist, sliding my fingers into her cunt. It would be wet for me, impatient, eager, and painfully swollen.

"Why are you looking at me like that?" she demands.

The thread of fear in her voice makes my eyes snap back to hers. She is white and trembling with rage, but at the expression on my face, she takes an involuntary step backwards only to come up against the bed. I tower over her, as I've always done, but this time it is not just physically that I will dominate. This time I am in full and total control ... and she is going to serve me with everything that she has.

"What do you want?" she spits. "Is it money? I'll get it for you."

The offer is insulting. As if I'd take even a red cent off her. I pull out my cell phone from my pocket and toss it over to the bed. "Call your father," I instruct.

She stares defiantly at it. "How much do you want?"

"Everything he owns."

Her head shoots up, a scowl of disbelief across her face. "What kind of stupid kidnapper are you? Who asks for everything? Trust me, my father is not going to give you everything in exchange for me. He has three other children to think of."

I manage to keep the dark smile at bay, but she is oh, so entertaining. The excruciating wait for her has been worth it. "Oh, but I intend to take everything he has."

"Are you out of your mind?" she sneers. "If it is that easy to become so bloody wealthy then why does anyone need to spend their whole life busting their ass to make something of themselves, you fucking loser."

She has a fucking dirty mouth on her. On any other girl, it would have turned me off instantly, but on her it makes me want to sit down and just fucking listen to her disrespect me. She goes on with her torrent of insults. The girl has absolutely no sense of self preservation. And she is unbelievably arrogant. This part of her I absolutely loathe.

"How much do you bloody want?" she repeats, snatching up the phone. Either anger has made her forget her initial fear, or she completely read me wrong. She thinks she can use bluster to dominate me. I am not her gardener's son anymore. I am her master.

"If you say the wrong thing," I say quietly, as she begins to dial his number, "he will be dead before the sun rises."

She freezes then and watches me with shocked eyes as I cross my arms across my chest. "Right now, your father is in a meeting near Hammersmith station. He is, however aware that you have gone missing so you can tell him that you have been whisked off to Spain by some of your friends for your upcoming birthday. And that you will be back soon."

She watches me carefully and I see the realization come into her eyes. She knows now I mean every word of what I am saying.

"He will never believe that," she replies slowly. "I just started a job that I've been looking forward to all year. Today is only my first day, he will never believe that I have suddenly decided to take off."

"Then concoct your own story. For his own good you better make it a believable one. If he is alarmed, and goes looking in the wrong places, the picture of his corpse might be the last thing you ever see of him."

I see the moment true terror comes into her eyes, all the color instantly draining from her face.

"What do you want with me?" she asks. "He'll give you all the money you want, just let me go."

"I have my own money." I reply.

She frowns. "Then what do you want?"

"*You. You are* what I want."

Her suspicions of exactly how I want her is as clear as day in her eyes. "You're sick," she hurls at me, color flooding up her neck and making her cheeks bloom.

"That is the general consensus," I agree pleasantly.

"Are you going to take me by force?"

I smile at her choice of words. *Take me by force*. Well, well, what an interesting thought. Still … "No, I'm not going to do that. I want your total and complete obedience. I want you to open your legs when I tell you to, and suck my cock when I need relief."

I say nothing and she makes her declaration. "I'll kill myself before I let myself become your fuck toy."

I think of the crudest thing I can say. "That's okay." I flash a sick smile. "I'll just fuck your corpse. I don't need you alive to enjoy your body."

Tears pool in her eyes, and for the first time she seems fragile and vulnerable. It doesn't last long though. She straightens her spine and furrows her eyebrows even deeper. "Why do you hate me so much? What have I ever done to you? I don't even know you. Have you thought you might have the wrong girl?"

"The wrong girl? That's funny," I sneer, a laugh rolling out of me.

"You're mad," she snarls.

"I am," I respond. "So you better not test me. Make the call, *now*."

CHAPTER FIVE
Liliana

*T*urning my gaze to the phone in my hand, I wonder if I will even be able to use it. I cannot even feel it anymore.

Somehow, I find myself dialing the only number I know by heart and only because my father made all his children learn it by heart so we could call him even if we didn't have our cellphones. I lift the phone to my ear as it begins to ring. It is answered immediately and my dad's voice rushes into my ear.

"Hello," he barks urgently. He must know it is me, because no one except our family members have this number.

I take a shaky breath before I speak. "Daddy," I say, and it is unbelievably difficult to keep my voice from breaking down and begging him to fix everything for me, the way he has always done. For all of us.

"Where the hell are you? It's almost four in the morning and you're not back at your apartment. The last time you were spotted was at a bar." His voice sounds very quiet, which usually means he is furious, but strangely I feel that underneath the veneer of rage he is terrified out of his mind at the thought of what might have happened to me.

I swallow and speak carefully. "You fixed it for me at Osborne and Nesbit, didn't you?" I accuse. "That's why they accepted me."

For a few seconds there is dead silence, then he fires back, his voice incredulous, "And so what? What has that got to do with you disappearing for hours?"

The tears fall from my eyes then for the parents who love me so, so dearly that they would do anything for me. Both of them must think I am so selfish to disappear without a word for something so stupid. I square my shoulders. Let them think whatever they want of me, my remit is clear. I will protect my father with everything I have. My voice breaks as I speak. "I told you I wanted to try to make it for myself, and now you've gone and ruined it all."

"All I did was get you in," he bites out. "What happens afterwards and how far you go is all up to you."

"That's not true, not anymore. What happens now and how far I will go will all depend on your name, and not me," I pretend to yell.

"Liliana," he calls, "Where are you?"

"They kept hounding me," I babble, "because they know I am your daughter. All I wanted was a few months working as myself and you've spoilt that for me."

"Liliana what is the matter with you?" he asks, his voice sounds strangely desperate. I've never heard him sound so.

I wipe the tears from my eyes and sniff miserably. "I've left the apartment. I need to think and clear my head. I'll be back after my birthday."

"After your birthday?" he echoes in disbelief. "Don't you want to come home for your birthday? Even if you are angry with me, don't you want to see Mum? Your sister and your brothers?"

Even the mention of Mum makes me feel panicky and frightened. What if she has another breakdown? I try to speak, but I can't. My throat feels choked.

"Liliana, are you still there?"

"Is Mum there, Dad?"

"No, she's at home, out of her mind with worry. I'm in London looking for you."

"Oh, Dad," I sob.

"Where the hell are you, Liliana?" Dad demands suddenly.

My heart jumps in my chest. When I was young, I used to tell the most terrible lies, but when I was ten years old after I told a lie that almost caused Dad's horse to die, my father made me promise that I would never lie to him again. No matter what he wanted the truth from me. From that moment onwards I have never lied to him. "Spain," I whisper.

He flares up. "Hell, Liliana. How dare you leave the country without informing me? Have you no thought at all for your own safety?"

"I need the time away, Dad. I need to think about what I want to do with my future. I'll call you again in a few days. Since you are in London can you go over to my apartment and pick up Moose. I couldn't bring him, so he's all alone in the house with no food or water. I know Mum won't mind taking care of him until I get back. He's missing Mum anyway." I swallow the lump in my throat.

"I've already been to your apartment. Moose is waiting in my car now," he says quietly, with not even a trace of reproach in his voice.

Relief floods through me. Thank God, Moose is not without food or water. "I'm really sorry, Dad ... but for once just let me do things my way."

"Whose number is this?" he asks suddenly.

My gaze flutters over to my captor's. He is staring at me his face, cold and unemotional. "Just someone I met."

"Where is your phone?"

"The battery died and I didn't bring my charger. Please don't try to track me, Dad. I brought cash with me so I won't be using any of my cards."

"What is going on, Liliana? You're smarter than this. Tell me exactly where you are and I'll fly down and get you," he says so quickly his words join together. It is as if he realizes that our call is coming to an end and he is panicking.

"I love you Dad with all my heart and I'm grateful for all you've done for me, more than you will ever know, but please, allow me to have this little time to myself. I'll never ask for anything else again. Please tell Mum that I love her very, very much too, and not to worry about me, because I'm just fine. I just need a bit of time to think. I'll try to call her in a few days. Bye, Daddy." With that I disconnect the call and my hands fall to my sides.

An applause awaits me as I return to the nightmare of my new reality. "You've outdone yourself," he says. "I always knew you were brilliant."

The phone starts ringing again and I don't even have to look to know it is my dad calling back. I throw the phone on the bed and look straight at him. "What now?"

He walks towards me, his stride unhurried, but with such menace and threat that I react without conscious thought. My leg takes a sideways step and my other leg follows. My legs are retreating of their own accord. The nearer he gets the quicker my legs move. Until my back connects with a wall. He smiles then, a crooked, glorious upturn of one corner of his lips that it surprisingly makes an unfamiliar thrill of desire run down my spine.

Oh God! I am losing my mind.

This is totally insane. I have *never* lusted after any man before. How could I possibly feel this way in the frightening situation I am in? The only thing I can think of to even remotely begin to explain my reaction would be the height-ened emotions of terror, shock, and confusion I have endured in the last few hours.

He picks up the ringing phone and returns his gaze back to mine. We stare at each other as he raises the phone above his head. His eyes seem to turn even darker, and I see then; he detests me wholeheartedly. With every cell in his being he *loathes* me. His lips twist into a sneer and I know he is seething, but what for exactly I am not sure. He moves his hand back, and both mine rush up instinctively to cover my face. A thin scream of terror bursts from my throat as the phone slams into the wall just beside my head. It smashes into pieces and falls to the floor. My heart pounds in my chest. I don't dare move.

"Now," he says quietly. "You'll wait until I am ready to use you." He turns away and walks out of the room.

CHAPTER SIX

Jake Eden

*T*he line goes dead in my ear. My mind runs like wildfire, I redial the number, but it just rings and rings. "Pick up, pick up," I urge desperately. I kill the call. I know she is not going to answer. I send a text. I tell her to call me back. We have code in our family. If ever anyone is in a position where they have been kidnapped or being held hostage they just have to say one sentence. I made all my children practice it again and again from the time they were old enough to speak.

Dad, I forgot to feed the dog. Can you feed it for me?

She didn't say those words. I gave her more than one opportunity to say it. And yet I know my gut is vibrating with instinct. I know something is wrong. Very wrong. I take out my other cellphone and call Lily.

She answers immediately. "Did you find her?" she asks, her voice so full of desperation my heart breaks. I remember another time. Her face, white, sweaty, and savage, looking up at me from the bathroom floor. "I lost our baby," she whispered brokenly.

I inject enthusiasm into my voice. "Yeah, she called."

"Oh God. Thank God. Oh, Jake, Oh God, I've been so worried. Thank God."

"Have they found Lil, Mum?" I hear my second daughter, Laura ask.

"Yes, yes, Dad found her," my wife says with a joyful, nervous laugh.

I close my eyes. My fist is clenched so hard I can feel the veins on my forearm popping. In the background, I hear Laura shout with relief. She says something I can't make out then my two sons join in the celebrations.

"Jake, are you bringing her back with you?" my wife asks.

"Well, I don't have her with me," I say evenly.

I feel the mood switch. "What do you mean?"

"Liliana is in Spain."

"What?"

"She was so upset I had spoken with Nesbit and asked him to consider her for the internship that she took off in a temper to Spain, but she must have come to her senses and called me to say she just wants some time to think things out on her own." Even to my own ears my explanation sounded like bullshit.

"Jake, are you lying to me?"

"No," I respond immediately. I imagine her standing in our

kitchen, the phone clenched in her hand. In the background my other children have stopped celebrating.

"Then I don't understand," she whispers. "Liliana went off to Spain without telling any of us because she was mad at you for putting in a good word in Nesbit's ear, is that what you are saying?"

"Yes, that's what she told me."

"I don't believe her. Do you?"

I stay silent.

"Give me her number. I want to call her," she demands, the fire coming back into her voice.

"What's going on, Mum," Caleb, our older twin asks.

She ignores him. "Jake, are you still there?"

I exhale slowly. "Darling, you can't call her. She doesn't want us to contact her. She wants a bit of time to think about her future, but she promised to call again soon."

"What about Moose? Did she take him?"

"No," I mutter. "She asked me to pick him up and bring him home."

"Jake, this is not how Liliana behaves. Something is wrong. I know something is wrong and I know you know it too. You're just not telling me." She starts sobbing.

"Lily, you have to stay strong. For Liliana's sake you have to. Whatever it is I will get to the bottom of it. I will find her and bring her back home. Do you hear me?"

She doesn't answer. Just carries on sobbing. I end the call, and suddenly the past flashes into my mind. I remember the first time I saw her. Oh, sweet baby Jesus, I thought I'd died and gone to heaven then. She was so damn beautiful.

Slowly, I unclench my hand and the blood rushes into my palm. I lift my head and look up at the night sky. "Where are you Liliana?" I whisper. The only thing I know for sure is: she is not in fucking Spain.

I make my promise then.

"I will find you if it is the last thing I do," I say to the dark moonless sky.

CHAPTER SEVEN

Liliana

For the next few hours I remain in the corner where he left me, crouched on the floor, my arms hugging my knees. The sun rises, filling the room with its pale light. Eventually, there are footsteps outside. More than one person is approaching. So, there are other people in this house. If I play my cards right, they could help me escape. I lift my head as the door is flung open.

A large man and a woman look down at me.

The woman looks to be in her mid-fifties. She is wearing a plain dark-blue dress and has a confident erect bearing. If I had to guess I would say she is the housekeeper. Even though her face is stern, her eyes are incredibly kind.

The man beside her is as brutish as a bull with thick shoulders, a low brow, and a military haircut. There is a blank expression in his narrow set eyes. I spot the gun he wears under his badly cut suit.

I rise on wobbly legs and focus my attention on her. "I'm here against my free will," I say in a shaky voice. "I've been kidnapped. I'm a prisoner here. Please, please, can you help me escape?"

The man snorts with laughter. A horrible sound.

The woman gives him a dirty look before walking up to me and smiling kindly. "You're not a prisoner, Lass. You're a guest in this house. I'm Mrs. Parks, the housekeeper, and I'm here to move you over to the main wing. There is a much better room set up for you there. Please come with me."

For a moment, I think about refusing or insisting I be set free, but it is clear that would be a pointless exercise. She wants to pretend I am a guest. Better if I follow her and find out as much as I can about where I am being held. Perhaps I can try and make friends with her and eventually persuade her to help me.

I expect them to blindfold me as they lead me away, or at least bind me up in some way, but I walk deceptively free out of the room. As if I truly am a guest.

We pass down corridors, and through open doors I see lavish rooms. As we approach an intersection with large windows I see that we are right in the middle of moorland. The windswept scenery is breathtakingly beautiful, but it also looks like we are very isolated in the harsh wilderness. There doesn't look to be another building as far as the eye can see. When we turn the corner though, I spot what looks like a farmhouse next to a lake in the distance. There is smoke coming out of its chimney. I file away that information and an escape plan begins to hatch in my head.

We enter the adjoining wing and it is almost as though I have stepped into a different world. The main house cannot be described as anything but palatial. Tall ceilings full of frescos, massive chandeliers, tapestries, gilded paintings, pillars, and gorgeous milky statues.

He had not been joking when he said that he had his own money. Which made the notion of my kidnap as some kind of revenge staggeringly baffling. Why would anyone with this kind of money hold a vendetta against me? I have done absolutely nothing wrong to anyone. I have barely even begun my life.

There is only one explanation: I am not the intended target.

Even though the hate I had seen my captor's eyes was clearly very much personal and directed at me, my capture had to be something to do with hurting my father. Even as a child I was already aware my father was unlike any of the other kids' mild-mannered fathers. Dad's circle and influence ran dark and deep. In all the high value dealings he has had over the years he's almost definitely gained many an enemy. It makes perfect sense. Attacking me is more brutal than going directly for my father.

We tread through galleried corridors, pass three massive lounges, a sun-drenched breakfast room, and eventually arrive at a foyer dominated by a gigantic chandelier. I come to an abrupt standstill. How absolutely bizarre. The whole place is uncannily similar to the one at my father's home. Down to the heavy centerpiece of tulips on a black granite stand. I look around me in a daze as we move toward the grand black marble staircase.

Mrs. Parks climbs the stairs and I follow. The bull stays behind me, a very permanent scowl etched into his face. The curving staircase takes us to a landing with a massive stained glass window. A short walk down a red-carpeted corridor and Mrs. Parks stops and turns towards me.

"This will be your bedroom." She opens the door in front of her and looks at me expectantly.

At this point the bull-like man turns around to take his leave as though his work of escorting us has been completed as I step into the room.

"Isn't it nice?" Mrs. Parks asks cheerfully from behind me.

The room is impeccably decorated in rich shades of forest green, teal, peacock blue, and accents of burnished gold. It is obviously the work of a very talented designer. The walls are covered in luxury wallpaper and the curtains are emerald green and gold brocade. An intricately carved bed sits on, what seems to be, a luxurious cream silk carpet.

"What would you like for breakfast, lass?" Mrs. Parks asks. "I dare say I could rustle up anything you desire."

I turn to her in confusion. This is not how a kidnapped victim should be treated. "I have been drugged and kidnapped and brought here against my will. Why am I being served as if I am a guest?"

I see pity in her eyes before she masks it. "He isn't as bad as you think. Just be patient and all will be well," she whispers softly. "I'll send up a tray with a selection of dishes." Then she turns around and takes her leave.

The door is shut and locked behind her.

For how long I stare at it, I don't know, but eventually, I push aside the turmoil in my head and go in search of the bathroom. A painful bump of my head hitting the tiled wall jerks me awake. Incredible, but I fell asleep on the toilet seat. It must be a lingering effect of the drug. I shake my head to push away the last webs of sleep, and think about taking a shower. It would wake me up and make me feel less filthy.

On the marble top I find everything has been set in place, toothbrushes, soap, towels. Locking the door, I shower as quickly as I can before washing my underwear in the sink and hiding it behind the used towel on the rack to dry. Regretfully, I have to put my old clothes back on, which smell of onions and sardines now. Unlocking the door, I return to the bedroom. There is another door in the room. Out of curiosity I try it.

Inside the walk-in closet are rows upon rows of clothes hung on display for me. There are shelves with dozens upon dozens of designer purses, some of them I already own. Underneath them is an impressive assortment of high heeled shoes.

I find it impossible to believe that they are really meant for me so I quickly grab a shoe to check its size. Six and a half: my exact fit. I check some others and they are all the same size. There is a dresser by the corner so I hurriedly pull out its drawers to see stacks of underwear and bras all in my size.

My eyes take in the underwear present and as I slam the drawer closed a bone chilling fear fills my belly. They are all of different patterns and colors, but there is one similarity between them all. They're all thongs. I take a step back and cast my eyes over the shoes and the clothes and I notice something I had missed before: they are all what a hooker would wear.

He wants to turn me into a prostitute.

His words the previous night come back to me. *It doesn't matter I'll fuck your corpse, I don't need you to be alive.* I collapse on the floor as every ounce of strength I possessed dissipates into nothing.

Someone knocks on the door and I whirl around and run back out to my room. The knock comes again. The sound is respectful so it must be one of the maids with my tray of food. I shout out that I am not hungry and wait until I hear her footsteps fade away. Slowly, I walk back to the bathroom. My underwear is dry and with a small sob that I cannot contain I pull them on and walk to a corner in the room. From here I can safely survey the whole room.

You'll be fine, Liliana, I console myself, but even I don't believe this. The tears come harder and harder until my throat turns sore, and my head feels like it is being pounded with a hammer.

CHAPTER EIGHT

Brand

https://www.youtube.com/watch?v=My2FRPA3Gf8

I find her crouched in a corner, her head down and her shiny hair covering her face, shoulders and arms. A voice screams with horror in my head. What have I done to my dream? Bile surges into my mouth. I take a deep, painful breath, my heart is pumping so hard I hear the blood rushing in my ears. I loom over her, angry and confused by my reaction to finding her in that condition. I tell myself I have no feelings for her but revenge. I will only have sex with her, because she owes it to me, but after that I will discard her with less emotion than a man flushing away a used condom after he has lain with a prostitute.

I watch her for a few seconds. She looks fragile and pitiful. I immediately harden my heart. It is just a trick of the light. She was a spoilt brat then, and now she is nothing but a rich bitch whose legs I will be spreading. There is an armchair by the window. I pull it with me, the wooden legs dragging against the hard wood floors.

The sound jerks her awake.

I station the chair about ten feet away from her. As I take my seat she jumps up and stands with her feet planted shoulder length apart in the flight or fight mode. I don't miss the terror in her eyes. Good. It strokes the part of me that needs to see her groveling and without an ounce of dignity. Just as my father had been years ago.

Yes, it is befitting she should fear me. I hold her life in my hands. I could just as easily stroke her delicate white neck, as break every one of her goddamn fingers.

Brushing her hair out of her eyes, she straightens her clothes and leans against the wall. She has cleaned up, I can see. Her face is completely devoid of makeup from the previous day, and it strikes me how much she still looks like she did nine years ago. Fresh eyed, pale, and fiery. Once I had thought her as beautiful as an angel.

But I was a boy then. A fool who didn't know better.

I keep my eyes on her, and watch her confidence begin to slowly dissolve into nothing. Still, she puts steel into her spine, lifts her chin, and speaks. "What do you want?"

I smile slowly. "I heard you once wanted to become a novelist. I have a story for you."

She says nothing, her brow furrowing with confusion.

"Don't you recognize me, Liliana?" I ask pleasantly.

She regards me, searching, her scowl deepening. My hands close into fists. She must remember me. She must. Then the light of recognition comes to her eyes. They widen in disbelief. Her jaw drops.

Time slows down for me. The seconds tick with excruciating slowness, but she refuses to give me any satisfaction. She doesn't admit remembering me. What a bitch! I grab the ash tray on the table and fling it across the room. It misses her head by a few inches and shatters into pieces.

She screams.

"I asked you a bloody question." This through gritted teeth.

"I don't," she yells.

I know that it is a lie. What did I expect from Jake Eden's daughter? Like father like daughter. I unclench my fists. I have to control myself. I can't let her get the better of me. With a soft laugh I lean back into the chair and stare mockingly at her. "Alright then. I'll tell you my story, perhaps it will help you ... remember."

She clasps her hands together so tightly her knuckles show white.

"Once I too had a family," I begin, spreading my knees and making myself comfortable. "One no less precious than yours. My father was a gardener and we lived in a caravan, like all the gypsies before us. We never stayed in the same place for more than a few months at a time." My face curls into a sneer. "If we did the pigs would come and move us along, anyway." I stop. "Wait ... that's not poetic enough, is it?"

Even from across the room I can almost hear her breath quicken with tension and anxiety.

"I'm not making my family sound very special. I apologize." I raise my eyes to the ceiling. What can I say to make us worthy of an Eden's attention?"

Her eyes are on mine, her attention complete, she is glued to my story. She almost doesn't blink.

"My mother had long black hair and bright green eyes. She was very beautiful. The strongest best men in our clan wanted to marry her, but she chose my father. I remember she used to crush up the geraniums my father brought home, and use it to rouge her cheeks."

She frowns. I thought that would get to her. "It is hard to forget such a woman. Would you forget her, little Liliana?"

She doesn't respond, and my brow begins to crease, which alerts her that she is displeasing me. She immediately straightens and responds. "I ... yes, I would. But what does she have to do with me?"

My gaze darkens at her dumb answer. I feign casualness, even though my gut is burning. "I thought I would tell you about her since you already know my father."

Silence.

My hand tightens on the armchair, as I voice my next question in an angry snarl, more animal than human. "You do know him ... don't you?"

Her hand moves to touch her head and she nods. Slowly.

My lips twist into a bitter smile. "Good. We're getting somewhere finally." Suddenly I don't want to play games anymore. I can't even look at her. There are things my heart misses that I can't share with anyone. I stand. "Funny thing about this story ... I'm almost never able to tell it in one sitting. We'll continue another time."

She takes a nervous step forward, her eyes wide and sparkling like blue stars. "Please ... let me go. I was just a child."

I frown. "Save your excuses I am not interested."

"What do you want with me?" she asks fearfully.

"I'm not sure, yet," I reply truthfully, as I turn and start to walk away. With the ghosts of my parents so nearby I have lost my desire for her.

"You've kidnapped me and hold me hostage in the middle of nowhere and you're not sure what you want?"

I stop and turn slightly. Her pose is defiant, but her eyes burn holes of fear in her pale face. The blood pounds in my ears. All these years I thought of her simply as a grain of sand in my eye. Easy to wash out, but she is not. She has disturbed all the devils and demons and ghouls that have gathered in my soul.

"All right, I'll tell you what I do know," I mutter. "I know between you and your father, I want one of you dead, and the other living with the guilt of that death over their head forever." I suck in my breath at the tough dilemma as I stroke my chin. "I just don't know though whom should die and whom should be tormented with the fact. Could you help me choose?"

She snaps then. Screaming like a banshee and clawing her hands, she rushes towards me. I catch her small wrists easily. She tries to kick at my legs, but I rush her backwards until her back hits the wall and winds her. She gasps with surprise and pain. Her breath is like a hot wind carrying old memories of roses, greenery, and the dark soil my father dug up. I press my body into hers to stop her from struggling, and instantly I become as hard as a rock.

She feels my erection and becomes still. Neither of us move.

I stare into her eyes and smell the soap on her skin, her shampoo. I feel the precious life-force inside her body and the heat from her skin. I hear her heart beating and the blood rushing in her veins. The lust hits me like a sucker punch in the gut. The need to spread open her legs and taste her is unbelievable. I have waited for so long. Why should I wait one second longer?

"Why should any of us die?" she whispers. "What the fuck did we do that was so wrong to you?"

"Because I swore I would avenge their deaths."

Her eyes pop open. "What is all of this about? I don't even know what you are talking about."

"It's all about guilt. It's about making you feel what I felt. I want to share my guilt with you, but how can I properly do that if you don't know what it feels like to cause the death of someone you love?" I let go of her.

Her legs refuse to keep her up and she slides down the wall into a heap on the floor.

I look down on her. "I think that answers my earlier question. Your father should be the one to die ... then you, just like me, you will live with the guilt."

She shakes her head, then looks directly into my eyes. "No, let it be me. It was my fault. Kill me instead."

CHAPTER NINE

Liliana

Nine years ago

I looked at the grubby boy. He was tall and broad with fierce black eyes and straight black hair. He must have been at least a couple of years older than me. He was the son of one of the traveling gypsies. His father did some work for my father. He was standing alone and staring into the pond. His clothes are dirty and his hands are black with dirt, but for some strange reason I couldn't understand I felt drawn to him. I decided to walk up to him and offer him some food.

"What's your name?" I asked, as I drew up to him.

"None of your business," he muttered, without even looking at me.

"What a rude little boy you are," I said scornfully. "I only came over to see if you are hungry."

"I'm not hungry. I don't need your charity."

I put my hands on my hips feeling angry at his rudeness. "I was only trying to be nice."

He turned to me his eyes flashing. "You want to be nice?"

I looked at him, confused. "Well, I did. I'm not sure I want to anymore."

"Then piss off."

I gasped in surprise. I didn't know why I didn't just walk away and tell Daddy, but I felt compelled to stay and fight him. "Why are you being so rude?"

"Why are you being such a pest?"

I crossed my hands over my chest. "Fine, I want to be nice. What do you want?"

He grabbed me so fast I yelped like a kicked puppy. Then before I knew what was happening he kissed me right on the mouth! I was too shocked to resist. His mouth was firm and forceful and hot. The kiss went on and on and to my surprise a little butterfly started fluttering in my belly. Then he lifted his head and looked into my eyes. I couldn't look away. I was too astonished.

"Liliana Eden, I'm going to marry you one day," he declared, before striding away.

I touched my lips. They were still tingling.

He kissed me.

Ewww ... Yuck.

The rude boy kissed me! I ran towards our house as fast as I can. I flew in through the front door and burst into the kitchen. Both Mummy and Daddy were there. "A boy kissed me," I announced breathlessly.

"What?" Dad shouted. He jumped up, his face dark with fury.

Mum grabbed hold of his wrist. "She's only eleven, Jake. It doesn't mean anything."

"Fuck it doesn't." Dad swore furiously as he strode out of the house.

I watched him march up to the boy's father. They talked, Dad gesturing angrily. The man called his son and slapped him upside the head. The boy said nothing. He just turned his head and looked at me through the window. There was no smile on his face. He just stared at me until his father slapped him again and pulled him away.

I touched my lips. They were still tingling. I wished now I had not told Dad about the kiss.

CHAPTER TEN

Brand

I narrow my eyes in feigned contemplation. "Hmm. The only thing your father is guilty of is treating my father and I as lesser than dogs. You on the other hand ..."

I can never say it out loud, or even admit it to myself how much she affects me. My gaze roves down her body, at the full breasts accentuated by her posture on the floor and straining against the material of her blouse, the slim waist, and the gently flaring hips. The ache for her is almost painful. I lower my hand and grab the hardened rod between my legs.

At the sudden fear in her eyes, I smile slowly. Reaching down I pull her to her feet. "Look at you, all grown-up and at the mercy of the lowly gardener's son."

She does a strange thing then. She licks her lips. I've been around the block too many times to know it was not a dry mouth that made her do that. Astonished, I brush my thumb along her wet bottom lip. The flesh is soft and plump. "Have you ever thought of me, Liliana?"

For a second she hesitates, then she shakes her head.

What did I expect from the daughter of a criminal? I let go of her. "Grab that chair," I order, jerking my head towards another chair close to her, "and pull it with you back to your corner."

She stares at me red-eyed, as though not understanding me. When I don't repeat myself, but my gaze darkens, she jerks into action. She drags the chair on the hardwood floors making the same scraping noise I had used to wake her up.

"That's perfect," I say, sitting down on the chair I had pulled to the middle of the room. "Now, take off your clothes."

She stares at me in horror and for a split-second I expect her to fall to her knees and plead with me again. Instead, she lifts her chin haughtily and asks, "Will this save my father?"

I shrug. I'm glad she didn't beg. "It's a start."

With her eyes on me she lifts her hands and begins to slowly undo the buttons of her blouse. When every button is undone, she shrugs it off her shoulders. Her movements unsexy, but unhurried as though she is either hoping her strip-tease is so fucking boring I will lose interest, or I will suddenly find my conscience and ask her to stop. Unfortunately for her there is no chance of either scenario happening. With every button that she releases my body becomes more and more taut with primal desire. By the time she is down to her dark lace bra I cannot take my eyes off her breasts. She pauses.

"Take it off," I hear myself growl.

Swallowing audibly, she does as she is told. To hide her expression she lowers her head, before she reaches behind and unsnaps the scrap of lace. Her breasts are revealed—creamy red-tinged beauties.

"Carry on," I urge thickly, my eyes moving down her cinched waist and past her belly button. The panties she is wearing cover too much. I hate it. "There's a whole drawer of underwear that I have provided. From now on you either wear those or nothing at all."

She doesn't respond.

Fuck her. I lay out my next instruction. "Take your underwear off, then spread yourself open and hang your legs from the arms of the chair."

Now I have her attention. She gasps and opens her mouth as if to argue, but all I have to do is raise my eyebrows and say, "Is your body worth more than your father's life?"

She closes her mouth with a snap and slips the offending material from her hips.

Ah, I knew she would be like this. Either waxed or freshly shaved, but as smooth as a baby's butt. My mouth is dry. She turns towards the chair giving me a great view of her full, round buttocks. My breath catches as she sits down and lifts her legs, one after the other, and hooks them on the arms of the upholstered frame.

Her cunt opens up like a beautiful, dew-coated flower, glistening with arousal. It is exactly how I imagined it would be: pink, and wet, and undeniably seductive. I hold onto the chair to keep myself from diving straight for her. I want her in my mouth, then I want my cock stretching her out and fucking her brutally.

I lean forward in uncontainable excitement and raise my

entranced gaze up to hers. "Do you ever fantasize about anyone?"

She doesn't respond just as I knew she wouldn't. Her gaze is blank and staring somewhere above my shoulders.

I go on. "Well, I have. Of you. Ever since I found you again two years ago. It was at a charity event. Your father was being honored and your whole family was there at the main table. Your skirt was so short you couldn't bend down. I overheard one of your brothers mocking you for it. Your hair almost reached your waist, shame you went and cut it, and your lips were bright red. I've been fucking you in my head ever since. And now here you are before me, open and exposed." I smile, teeth on full display.

Her eyes dart to mine in shock.

"Touch yourself," I command. "Put me in your mind," (*and heart*) the whisper comes from nowhere into my head. For a split second it stuns me, then it makes me mad. She is already trying to wrap me around her little finger. It won't work. I hate her. "And touch yourself," I order harshly. "Put on a show for me, Liliana. Behave like a whore for me."

Her eyes widen in disbelief.

"Is there a problem?" I enquire pleasantly, while thoroughly enjoying her humiliation the way she had once enjoyed mine. I need to escape from the torment and guilt that hangs over my head endlessly like a curse.

The silence seems to drag on forever as the angry tears once again fill her eyes, but the fury in them is also not overshadowed. She shuts her eyes as her hand begins to move towards her cunt and a burst of anger shoots through me.

"*Open your fucking eyes,*" I roar.

She recoils from the sudden outburst, her eyes snapping open.

"Don't make me tell you again," I remind her, leaning back against the chair.

Her gaze stays on me as her fingers inch towards her beautiful cunt. My mouth starts watering, my breathing is quietly ragged, and my cock threatens to burst out of my underpants. Outwardly, though, I remain calm, almost casual, as I watch her.

What is it about her?

Why does she alone have this tremendous effect on me? I am twenty-four years old, but I feel as if I have lived for a hundred years. During that time I have lost count of the number of women I have fucked to exhaustion. Not one compares to the excitement of seeing Liliana Eden, naked, and opened wide right in front of me.

"Palm yourself," I instruct.

Her hand covers her wet flesh.

"Press harder." I have to fight to contain the growl of the monster inside me. When she obeys, I see her juices well up between her fingers and run down. A chuckle of satisfaction passes my lips at the pretty sight. She wants this as much as I do. "Take your hand to your mouth and taste yourself."

Her defiant eyes condemn me. They tell me she will never forgive me for what I am doing to her. She doesn't know it turns me on even more ... to force her.

Bringing her hand to her lips, she sticks her tongue out and tastes herself. Although, she deliberately affects a bored expression, it is unconsciously sensual. Enough for my lips to part with thirst. I've been holding my breath without real-izing it. "Lick your fingers clean, slowly ... one after the other. Don't make me remind you to keep your eyes on me."

She follows my instruction, licking away the creamy moisture on her hand.

"You must be very aroused, your clit is so fucking swollen." I lift my gaze to hers, a satisfied smile on my face. Bright color fills her cheeks. "Stroke it," I command. "Hard and fast."

She begins to flick the pink bud. It is as clear as day in the tightening of her jaw, and her quick shallow breaths that she is fighting the pleasure.

I lean forward. "Faster."

She increases her movements, and in spite of herself, her hips begin to writhe. Her chest starts rising and falling rapidly, revealing the heightened pace of her heart. Her eyes become half-slits, with blue irises glittering between thick lashes. Soon her lust takes over. She gives up pretending to be unaf-fected and openly chases her climax to its conclusion. Her left hand grips the base of the chair to contain the violent bursts of desire coursing through her body. I watch her jerk and convulse, her breasts jiggling, with deep fascination. She is beautiful when she comes apart. It is a shame when she finally remembers where she is and the situation she is in. She forces her eyes open to look at me. There is utter contempt.

Showing such naked contempt is a mistake on her part. I hold all the cards.

"I'm afraid that was too brief," I drawl. "I want a full show. Please do it all again. This time imagine I am not here and don't be shy. Touch yourself better than any man ever can.

Squeeze your breasts, play with yourself, and fuck your own hole hard."

Her eyes widen and she swallows hard.

"You have fucked your own hole before, have you not, little Liliana?" I taunt.

"I have not," she denies breathlessly.

Yet another lie. "Should I come over then to teach you what you need to—"

"No!" she barks out immediately.

Her terror makes me laugh softly. I say nothing, just continue to gaze at her in her position of utter vulnerability and subjugation. "Well then impress me with what you can do to yourself."

She breathes easier when she sees that I'm not bent in my proposition to teach her. "I need to shut my eyes," she says, resentfully.

"You may," I concede with an amused smile.

Taking a deep breath, Liliana Eden shuts her eyes and begins. She takes her left breast in her hand and squeezes it gently. Her tongue slips out of her mouth and wets her bottom lip as her right hand pinches her reddish nipple, before slithering downwards. She rubs the swollen bud of her sex, and her clit is still so tender her ass almost lifts off the chair.

Her free hand tangles in her hair. The soft moans that fall from her lips make me want to shoot out of my chair and stick my tongue inside her. The tip of her finger eventually slips into her pink pussy and everything in me goes still. With my frame pushed forward, I watch as she gently digs in and out of herself.

"*Faster,*" I grunt, leaning forward.

She obeys, but her movements are uncoordinated almost as though she doesn't care. That infuriates me. I know she's no innocent. A beauty like her would have been with dozens of men so why is she deliberately behaving in this clumsy way?

I don't even realize I've shot out of my chair until it crashes backwards. Her eyes pop open and a small startled scream escapes her lips as she tries to scramble away. My chest feels like it is on fire. I catch her by the waist and bodily lift her slender frame off the chair, her limbs flail in the air.

"Let me go," she cries, but her struggles barely register on me. When she realizes she is no match and her movements are causing more friction between our bodies, she stops struggling.

I sit her back on the chair. With my hands on either side of it I lower my frame to stare directly into her eyes. "Are you testing me?" I ask, my voice dangerously quiet.

She is breathing heavily, her chest heaving hard, but she shakes her head. As I continue to stare into her eyes I feel her slowly begin to submit. Without taking my eyes off hers I spread her legs roughly apart and hook them back over the arms of the chair.

I grab her mound, the slick wet folds spreading out at my touch. Her juices soak my fingers. At that moment I would have given up my entire fortune to taste her. I want nothing more so I drop down to my knees, my hand against her to hold her in place, and cover her pussy with my mouth.

It is like coming home!

As I suck her cream into my mouth, my teeth nibble eagerly at the white bud protruding from its pink hood. It has been tormenting me from across the room and it is a relief to take it into my mouth. In between dirty curses and furious cries of shame and humiliation she writhes and groans with pleasure.

At one point she tries to push me away, but I am impossible to budge. Without releasing her clit, I plunge my fingers into her. Her head falls back when I start finger fucking her, pumping in and out so fast my fingers are a blur.

I hear her struggling to breathe as she thrashes fiercely against me, but I lost the ability to empathize a very long time ago. Sadistically, I keep thrusting into her until she quivers uncontrollably. Her hands claw in my hair, as her teeth sink deep into my shoulder in an effort to make me stop, but her body speaks a different language, writhing ferociously in tandem to the onslaught of my fingers.

She only releases my shoulder when she explodes in a powerful rush of passion, her body bowing, her mouth opening in a scream, as the first burst of her cum splashes into my mouth and face. It runs down my throat, and soaks my shirt.

Her climax is so strong she becomes unaware of herself. Strands of hair are glued to her forehead, her breasts are up in the air, and her mouth locked in a wide open O. Unthinkingly, she grabs my hand and holds on to it, pressing herself hard against me to relieve the torrent of ecstasy still shaking her to her very core. Mesmerized by the intensity of her climax I can only stare.

Then, overcome by emotion, helpless tears seep out of her half-closed eyes.

I rise to my feet and look down at her as she fights to catch her breath. She is a beautiful mess. Her eyes fly open and she stares at me with hatred. Her eyes slide away from mine contemptuously and drop to my fingers. What she sees makes her blink and I quickly follow her.

There is pink blood on my fingers!

I freeze with shock as my brain refuses to accept the evidence of my eyes. It is impossible. The spoilt rich bitch cannot possibly be a virgin at 20 years of age? In an instant, she shoots to her feet and strikes such a hard slap across my face it makes my head jerk violently to the side.

"Happy now, you sick bastard?" she spits.

She is trembling, her eyes filled with a hurt that, strangely, my frozen heart can feel. I turn away from her as tears start running down her face. I can't look at what I have done. My chest hurts. Shocked and confused, I start to walk away, but with a howl of fury she comes at me, and starts striking my back with all of her might.

I let her rain her clenched fists on my body. It actually feels good. I deserve to be punished. When I feel her blows lose their momentum, I turn around, seize her wrists, and throw her on the bed. She is as light as a feather. Standing over her, I watch her bounce slightly on the bed, her breasts bouncing. I haven't sucked them yet.

I stare down at her. She is like a wild animal. Her face swollen and blotched with crying, her chest is heaving, and her eyes glare murderously at me, but her young body is silently calling out to me. I bend down and, grabbing her ankles, open her legs wide. She doesn't struggle. She lets me. I look down at her abused pussy.

I will be the first man inside her.

I want her so bad it fucking kills me to turn away, fling her legs away, and walk out of the room. I slam the door shut and lock it. I feel like a mad man locking his treasure away. Because she is *mine* now. Even the thought of another man looking at her fills me with fire and rage. I will not rest until I have possessed her completely. Then I will fix it so no other man may touch her while I am alive. I stop at the unexpected thought. Where the hell did that come from?

Nothing is working out the way I planned.

CHAPTER ELEVEN

Liliana

For a long time after I hear the lock turn I remain naked on the bed, unmoving, my legs still open, staring at the ceiling. Not hearing or seeing anything. It feels like I am in a beautiful dream that suddenly turned into a nightmare.

The gardener's son. He has always brought both painful regret and a crazy warmth into my heart. Today, he brings indecipherable bafflement, disappointment, and hatred. I cannot believe that this is the man that I have pined over for years.

I thought of him incessantly, but never once have I ever contemplated I would be in a position like this. Or imagined it would be possible to be stripped to such a level of vulnerability and abuse. I feel like an animal. All these years in my head he was a Prince, in reality he is an unfeeling, feral beast. Not only am I a hostage, but I've just been sexually assaulted.

Then, a voice in my head speaks up. *Have you forgotten the shameless way you climaxed in front of him? When he opened your legs and looked down at your throbbing flesh, you wanted him to take you. You wanted to know what it would be like to have him inside you.*

I squeeze my eyes shut. I know that is the truth. I had no control over the way my body responded to him. And if it had been any other man it would have been unthinkable, demeaning and horrible, but because it was him, I don't even feel dirty. I don't even want to wash the smell of him away. Even though the sane, normal part of me wants to kill him for what he is doing to me and my family, the part of me that spent all these years yearning for that kiss wants him to come back and finish what he has started.

I think of the hatred in his eyes. He holds me responsible for the death of his father, but what exactly did I do that was so wrong? I thought back to that day almost a decade earlier. Over the years I thought about the incident incessantly, but not for the reasons he is now accusing me of.

I was angry at myself for running into the house and telling Dad about the kiss. It had been special until I opened my big mouth and told the world about it. I kicked myself for not being more like Mum. She would never have told a soul. Mum can keep a secret like nobody can. If only I had been just that little bit discreet everything would have been different. The gardener would not have been fired, both of them wouldn't have disappeared from our lives and whatever horrible thing had happened to his father might never have come to pass. In that one unthinking moment I changed the course of all our lives. And I never stopped regretting that careless move.

But that doesn't excuse his cruelty.

I was just a child and I could never have known the conse-quences of my childish actions. Even my dad firing his dad did not warrant kidnapping me and keeping me prisoner in the middle of nowhere and punishing me in this way. I think of my mother and how worried she would be to think of me alone in Spain. Thinking of her makes me tremble with fury. I close my legs. If my mother is in any way harmed, I am going to kill him, I swear it. I will hunt him down and kill the fucking bastard.

I rise to my feet then and head into the shower.

The water is scalding hot, but I don't feel a thing. I let the water wash him away. I am no longer a virgin. He doesn't know it but all these years I've been secretly saving myself for him. He is the only man in this world I've ever wanted. What a strange turn of events that my greatest dream was his ultimate revenge. I try to remember the kiss, but it has strangely become vague and colorless. As if it happened another lifetime ago.

It used to be so vivid and colorful. A kiss stolen on an innocent afternoon. The most exciting thing that had ever happened to me until then. I could remember everything, even recall the exact scent of him. A mixture of fresh sweat, earth, and something else.

If only ... if only the stars had aligned the way they should have and things had worked out differently.

But all I have now is the memory of his black eyes, how hungrily they roamed my body, and suddenly my hand slips down past my belly, to my core. I feel my breath quicken. The simple act of inhaling and exhaling becomes hard. I remember his hard finger inside me, rough, uncaring, intense. So intense nothing else existed but his fingers inside me.

No!

I pull away my hand violently, turn off the water, and stand with my head bowed. Water drips off my hair and runs down my body. Time passes. I don't know how long I stand there, but the steam in the air cools and goose pimples begin to scatter over my arms and legs. I start to shiver slightly.

And still the urge will not go away.

Tears of frustration fill my eyes. Fuck him! I slam my palms on the cold, wet tiles. My palm slides on the surface displacing water droplets. It moves lower. Suddenly it is off the tiles and between my legs. At the first contact with my clit a cry flies out of my mouth. I think of him. I cannot believe what I am doing. I cannot believe how animalistic is my lust and how little I knew myself. He doesn't need to lock me in. I hate him for what he is doing to me and my family, but I cannot run away from him any more than I can cut my heart out of my body.

My fingers begin to move faster and faster, but in my mind, they are not my own. They belong to him.

CHAPTER TWELVE

Brand

https://www.youtube.com/watch?v=lDpnjE1LUvE
-from the first day I saw her I knew she was the one-

$\mathcal{I}$ await her in the dining room south of the Manor. I knock back my glass of whiskey and slam it down on the eighteen-seater Italian rosewood table. My stomach is in knots. My housekeeper, Lindy Parks comes in and silently places a fresh drink in front of me, but the brief look she gives me is brimming with questions. The main one, no doubt. Why have I imprisoned a woman?

I ignore the look and she takes her leave.

I'm on my fifth whiskey when Liliana eventually strolls in, much, much later than I stipulated, but I cannot help the smile that spreads across my lips at her entrance. I requested she wear one of the dresses provided for her, however she has chosen to dress in the same soiled silk blouse and skirt she arrived in. Her face is free of any makeup, her hair severely secured at the back of her head, and her gaze is a glare of hatred.

"Take a seat," I invite, without standing up.

She goes and sits on the chair at the opposite end of the table.

I lean back into mine. "I requested that you be appropriately dressed." I glance down at my own ensemble of dark trousers and a crisp white dress shirt. "Even I made an effort."

"I like my own clothes," she says tightly.

I frown. "What is wrong with the clothes I have provided?"

"They are clothes fit for a whore. I'm not one."

I laugh softly. "Ah, but you are my whore. Do you want me to show just how much of a whore you are?"

Her eyes flash with panic. "No."

"Please ensure you dress in something different tomorrow."

She nods. "What is your name?"

"Brand."

"Brand Vaughan," she says softly.

"Yes, you remembered."

"I liked your father." Then she pulls out her weapon. "I too have a story to tell you. I was trying to help the gardener's son, but he had such a big chip on his shoulder he grabbed me roughly without permission and kissed me. What did he expect me to do?"

At her words, I instantly go still. Even as a boy I knew we were meant to be. It made me angry that she could not see it.

Leaning forward, I place both of my elbows on the table, and link my fingers together to glare murderously at her. "Liliana," I say. "Be *very* careful."

It is her turn to laugh. "Why? What are you going to do? Force me *again*?"

As calmly as I can, I push the chair back and rise from it. I want to walk away, but she refuses to let me leave.

She jumps to her feet and attacks me further with her accusation. "Is it not the truth?" she demands, and I stop in my tracks. "What then are you accusing me of? You said that I was the reason for your father's death, but the truth is you are the reason. If you had only controlled yourself that day he would still be alive now."

I feel the knots of fury within me begin to tighten dangerously. She is going to push me into killing her. "You really want to die, don't you?" I ask.

I see the fear flash instantly in her eyes, but her voice is strong and sure. "If killing me will bring you peace, then by all means do it, but first I need to know what exactly I did wrong? Why are you so hell bent on punishing me when you are as guilty as I am?"

I move, and in an instant I am on her, my hand encircled murderously around her neck. I knew she would push me too far. She claws at my hold as it chokes her, struggling to set herself free, and the more she struggles the tighter my hold becomes around her pale scrawny neck. Then tears come to her eyes. The moment I note them I feel a sharp shard of pain in my chest. It adds to the turmoil brewing in my heart.

I loosen my hold and see all the blood returning to her face. She lets her hand fall away and then croaks out, "I'm sorry, you are such a fucking child. You refuse to see that the real blame is all yours."

I cannot recall how it happens, but a flash of fury blinds me from coherency. I feel every nerve in me tighten and in the next moment she is on the floor and cowering in fear. I stare down at her in shock. Not certain what has startled me more. The fact that I almost hit her, or the feeling in my body. As if I just thrust a knife into my own gut and twisted it.

Turning around, overwhelmed by emotions that I can't understand, I feel myself stagger away. I have only gone a few steps when she bellows out my name.

"*Brand.*"

I come to an instant stop, but for what, I am not sure. A part of me wishes, hopes and even dares expect that she will somehow put me out of my misery. But how? Who can take this knife out of my flesh?

I turn back to look at her, still crouched on the floor. "I'm hungry. I haven't eaten since lunch yesterday."

For a second I stare at her in amazement, then my whole body reacts to her calm words. I forget to be angry or miserable. "Let's eat," I find myself saying, as I change course. I head over to my chair to take my seat and spread the napkin across my lap as if nothing has happened. I ring the bell and minutes later Lindy comes in with our starters. Silently, she starts to serve us. The food smells very good. I pick up my cutlery, but find I cannot eat a thing.

My gaze lifts and lands on her. She is tucking into her meal hungrily. While she is unconscious of my gaze she has no defenses up and she just looks young and innocent again. Like that girl I was smitten with so long ago. The one that I was determined to make mine, only I was so overwhelmed by my own feelings I came across as rude and horrible.

She looks up and her eyes catch mine. "What?"

"Nothing."

She butters a roll and carries on eating. Lindy comes to clear away the plates. "Was the food not to your liking?" she asks, a frown on her forehead.

"I'm not hungry." My voice is sharper than I intended.

Liliana lifts her glass of wine and takes a small sip. The room falls silent. Lindy brings in the main course. Confit of duck legs in port sauce. It is accompanied with buttered samphire, crushed potatoes, and finely sliced carrots.

Once again I can barely look at my food, but Liliana polishes off her plate. I'm surprised she doesn't lift it up and lick it clean. That brings to mind an eye-popping image. Lindy comes in to clear away the plates, and she pointedly does not mention my untouched food.

"Next up," she announces, "is chocolate pudding with raspberry sauce." It is her specialty and my favorite, but I decide to skip it. There is only one thing I want to eat. My swollen cock can no longer be ignored. "No. No dessert for us."

"But I wanted dessert," Liliana says peevishly.

"That will be all, Lindy. Go out and lock the door behind you," I murmur, not taking my eyes off my prey.

"Goodnight, Brand," Lindy says, and goes out of the door. The sound of the key turning echoes around the room.

"What now?" Liliana challenges, her eyes sparkling like gemstones.

"Now, I eat you," I say, rising.

She sees me coming and hastily gets to her feet. I expect her to try and escape, but instead she stands her ground, blood in her eyes. It turns me on even more, and by the time I reach her I am close to exploding.

In a moment her back is slammed against the table. I grab both of her thighs in my hands and jerk her legs open. Ignoring her curses I push her skirt up to get to her sweet cunt. Ripping off her goddamn grannie panties in one swift jerk, I pull her towards the bulge of my hard cock. I grind my hips brutally against hers, the groan arising from my throat raw and animalistic. My arms go around her protesting body to hold her in place and for a moment, as I try to catch my breath, it's almost as though I am holding onto her for dear life.

"Let me go, you big ugly brute," she says between gritted teeth.

My answer is to take a nip at her neck. Her breath comes out in a rush of excitement, before she catches herself and increases her resistance, but the more she fights the more aroused I become. Her puny struggles urge me to trace brutal kisses down her heated skin until I get to her chest. Once and for all I rip her shirt apart. There will be no more wearing this ugly piece of shit in my house.

The buttons fly in all directions as the shirt falls open. I make short work of her bra. One flick and I'm in. I yank it away to reveal her beautiful breasts. With one hand I grip both of her wrists and twist them behind her back so her breasts are exposed and pushed out towards me. I stop for an instant to take in the riveting sight, but in my moment of distraction she drops her head back and swings it furiously forward and head butts me.

A sharp pain shoots through my skull. I see stars and lose my grip on her hands. As I stagger backwards, I see her recoiling even worse from the blow. She holds her head in her hands to contain the pain.

I can't help the bitter, taunting laugh that flows out of my mouth. "This is rich. Your father is a Class A thug and that's the best you can do! You *have* been sheltered, haven't you? Jake Eden's little princess. So precious, I had to pay the greatest price for even daring to touch you. And all these years I've been dying to have you ... to see if you are indeed special."

I can feel my temper careening out of control once more so I look briefly away from her. By the time I return my gaze to her, she has her shirt pulled tightly in her hands to cover her chest.

"I'd rather die than let you touch me again," she declares, her face white.

"Go ahead," I encourage callously. "There's a knife on the table next to you. You should know how to make it work. You are Jake Eden's daughter, after all."

With her eyes on me she does as I have suggested. I watch her hand slant as she brings the one edge of the knife to the base of her throat.

I laugh as I move closer to her. "That's the blunt end, sweet-heart. You'll be a long time dying that way."

Suddenly, with a cry of fury, she swings the knife in my direction. I jump back and evade the blade, but she manages to slash the sleeve of my shirt. I look down. I had not felt any pain, but blood seeps through the white material. I look up at her and smile softly. "There, I drew your blood this afternoon, and now you've drawn mine. As such I can get down to the business of fucking you."

She swallows hard, then places the sharp end of the knife across her slender throat, and shuts her eyes. Her hands are shaking and I realize with a sharp pang of panic in my chest I have pushed her so close to the edge she might actually go through with it.

"Go ahead," I say to her as coldly as I can. "But just remember your father will join you shortly."

Her eyes shoot open.

"Deathcap Mushrooms," I say. "Have you heard of it?"

"There is not yet any known cure for this poison … it is one of these things if you ingest it … you die horribly as your kidneys and liver give up. A very painful and slow death."

She has become as quiet as death.

"I briefly considered taking him out with a bullet, but where is the retribution in that? Too quick. He deserves to suffer as I did."

Her hands begin to lower from her neck.

I cock my head as the thrill of sweet victory flows through my veins. "Have you changed your mind?"

She flings the knife away, then roughly jerks the shirt off her body, and chucks it away. "Alright then," she says coldly. "You want to have me, go ahead."

No words come to my head. For as long as I can remember I dreamed of this moment. Her complete capitulation.

"I was once incredibly attracted to you." She swallows hard. "I can't lie. I still am. Go ahead and fuck me Brand Vaughan. I will enjoy every single moment of it, I promise you. Let us both be out of our minds together. This is between you and me. Leave my family out of it."

My grin was from ear to ear.

CHAPTER THIRTEEN

Liliana

https://www.youtube.com/watch?v=uelHwf8o7_U

*H*is smile is sick.

The complete absence of humor in it makes me feel as if a reptile is slithering over my body. Even so, and unexplainably, I cannot deny how intensely my body is responding to his. I spent the whole afternoon telling myself I hate him and it is no good. One look at him and all I want to do is throw myself at him.

It is clear fighting him is not doing me any good. Short of somehow killing him, or myself and causing the demise of my father, I see no other way than to succumb to him. At least until I overcome my own madness, or a window of opportunity to escape arrives. Once I am away from him and close to my family again I am certain I will regain my sanity. I do however have one last question.

"Brand, can you really not see how unreasonable your need for revenge is? No matter what the unfortunate consequences were of my actions they were unintended. I was just a child. As you were. You can't possibly still be this angry and bitter because an eleven-year old child told her father a boy kissed her. What is the real reason why you are so bitter towards me?"

Just as I expected he doesn't respond.

It confirms my suspicion. "You do not know yourself, do you? What you do know however is that you cannot get me out of your mind, can you? You've been trying countless times over the years. So you've blamed me for everything ... your grief, and perhaps even your guilt for what happened to your father because of your desire for me."

He drops his head in barely restrained temper and I realize that I am getting to him. I go on.

"You want to kill me, but at the same time you want to have me. You cannot make up your mind and it's tearing you up, but one thing is for sure. You want to see me suffer ... just as you have."

He lifts his head then and I watch as his gaze slides over my breasts, the hunger in them evident, and then his eyes travel back up to mine.

Something cold grips my entire body. I am sure that I have finally lost my mind. Maybe the fear and terror has gotten to me, but despite everything in me screaming to hold on to that last bit of my dignity, I reach behind and unhook, unzip, and let fall my skirt. When it pools around my feet, I step out of it and stand before Brand buck naked in the middle of his grand dining room. I feel as if I am going to throw up, but I don't. I keep my composure and my gaze on his.

"Go ahead," I say to him steadily. Maybe this is the only response to the madness between us.

He stares at my body saying nothing.

"Where will you have me?" I demand. I look towards the expensive wallpaper, I know it is expensive, because my mother has it on her dining room walls too. "Against the wall?" I glance at the polished hardwood floor. "On the floor?"

When he doesn't respond I swing my head towards the expanse of the dining table. Purposefully, I head towards the middle, and with a long sweep of my hand, send the carefully arranged food and utensils to the ground. They crash to the floor, plates, cutlery, silver salt and pepper containers. The crystal decanter of red wine somehow manages not to break, but spills its precious contents on the floor and rolls in a circle. A magnificent porcelain vase smashes to pieces, scattering the flowers inside it haphazardly. The water runs quickly in all direction and mingles with the red wine. It is a fine mess I have made. My mother would be horrified.

I pop myself on top of the cleared table, and do the unimaginable. I spread my legs wide open.

Then I meet his gaze, my heart pounding so loudly in my chest, I can almost hear nothing else. He walks over to me, his stride unhurried, his eyes never leaving mine. When he is a foot away from me he stops. Very, very gently, he pushes two thick fingers into me. My mouth opens in a silent gasp. For a few seconds, his fingers remain still, then he withdraws them. He brings his fingers to my face and runs the wet pads of his fingers horizontally across one cheek then the other. As if he is painting the stripes that native American and certain indigenous tribes do to their faces.

"You were better when you were a Warrior Princess, wild and fierce," he says almost sadly.

Then he turns around and strides out of the room. The shame that comes down upon me in that moment makes me want to run away and never see him again. I am unguarded. I look out of the window. It is snowing lightly and I know I will not survive out there in my torn clothes. I do not know how I manage it, but somehow I get myself off the table, pick up my clothes, put them on and walk out of there as calmly as I can.

CHAPTER FOURTEEN

Liliana

The knock to my door almost makes me jump out of my skin.

It is either Brand or one of his other staff. I hear the key begin to turn and the decision is taken away from me. Shutting my eyes, I sink my head into the pillow and feign sleep.

Footsteps come in and stop for a moment before moving away from my bed, and towards the coffee table. There is some shuffling around and then eventually the clink of plates against each other. I lift my head and see that it is Mrs. Parks.

Her smile is welcoming as she calls me over for the meal that she has just laid out, but my reply is rude. "Go away and leave me alone."

"I just spent an hour on my hands and knees cleaning the dining room," she says, and I instantly feel bad. It is not her fault. I did not mean for her to suffer the brunt of my violent reaction to Brand. "You have to eat breakfast. Please join me."

As if on cue my treacherous stomach begins to growl in protest. "Thanks, but I'm not hungry."

She sits down and starts pouring coffee into a cup. "If I were you, I would keep my strength up. Who knows when you might need it." She takes a sip of coffee and looks at me over the rim of the cup.

I rise. "I'll brush my teeth first if you don't mind." After brushing my teeth, I join her on the couch.

She holds up a plate of finger sandwiches and I take my pick. White bread with scrambled eggs. The sandwich is gone in two bites. I reach out and take another with ham and tomatoes. It is delicious and before long I am going for a cucumber sandwich. I am even hungrier than I expected so it is only about midway through the meal that I lift my head and meet Mrs. Parks watching me as she chews in a very lady-like fashion. It is a bit unsettling after the way I have been making a pig of myself.

She immediately catches on to my discomfort. "There's already a lot to make you uncomfortable," she says apologetically. "I don't mean to add to it."

I stop eating and study her. She has genuine kind eyes, but along her graying hair, there are smile lines all over her face, or are they lines from hardship? She is my best bet of formulating any kind of escape or trying to find out more about Brand.

"I hope you don't mind me asking, but do you know Brand personally?" Or is he just your employer? It's just that he called you Lindy."

"Brand came into my life a long time ago, I think he was about fifteen at the time."

My heart catches in my throat as I realize that Brand was the same age when he left my father's employ. "How did you meet?" I ask, my tone more eager than I wanted to let on.

"I met him at a soup kitchen in South Ealing. He used to come in almost every morning and evening like clockwork. I was there for breakfast and dinner too so I didn't have much pity to give, but what struck me was how young he was. He was always dirty and unkempt, but one day he came in bruised and bloodied. I couldn't take my eyes off him."

She stops and sighs heavily at the memory. "You see he was always so surly and aggressive no one dared go close enough to ask him what had happened. I was the only one who walked up to his table and sat opposite him. I took my slice of bread and put it next to his bowl of soup. To my surprise tears rolled down his black and blue eyes. The tears never stopped. He cried so much that his soup doubled in size. He even cried while he ate." She worked up a smile at the joke but it was so sad that it instead made my heart ache.

She went on. "He hid it well, so no one else noticed but even if they had, every one of us in that place were at the lowest in our lives. Tears were the only currency we had … and we had them in abundance."

She laughed again and the shard in my chest dug deeper.

"Through all the tears he never said a word. When he had eaten the last spoonful, he got up and walked out, but that day I followed him. He went down the road, searching. I wondered what he was looking for. It was an especially freezing cold night and I was almost giving up with following him aimlessly looking at shop windows and sitting around on park benches, when I saw him finally stop at one of those

Biffa recycle dumpsters. I watched as he got into it and made his bed for the night."

My eyes widen. He was sleeping inside a dumpster.

"I couldn't take it anymore. I didn't have much, but I did have a floor in my own home that we could both share. I banged on the dumpster and told him I was there to help him and take him home with me. Of course, he rejected me. I'll never forget his eyes though. They were full of mistrust. There was no hope in them at all. All his belief in humankind was gone."

She smiles at me and the shard goes even deeper till it feels like I am starting to bleed on the inside. I know that I was indirectly responsible for this. I clear my throat and sit up. "How did you get him to go with you?"

"I told him that one of the soup kitchen regulars a while back used to sleep in dumpsters the same way he was doing. The disposal truck came however one early morning when he was deeply asleep, lifted the dumpster into the air, and crushed him to death." She grins. "I exaggerated the situation horribly, of course. I told him his intestines came out of his mouth and his brain came out of his ears."

I smile weakly at her.

"Dragging him along with me was hard work. A few times he tried to give me the slip, but I never let go. Since then, though, he's been the one to drag me along with him." She laughs then and rises to her feet. "Eat a bit more, dear," she says. "And get as much rest as you can."

The look she gives me is so apologetic that I can see she is telling me all this to atone in some way for his behavior.

There is no doubt he didn't tell her about the reason for my presence in the house, and perhaps the walls he set up just beyond their care for each other prevents her from asking.

Just as she reaches the door, I lift my head. "Can I ask you another question?"

"Yes, ask away."

"Why were you at the shelter?"

I have never seen someone's face fall so suddenly. She manages a smile and responds with tears in her eyes. "I used to be a nurse at St Mary's hospital down in Lambeth. After many years of being childless I became pregnant. My world lit up. Nothing could go wrong. My dream had come true until I went for a pre-natal care appointment and tested positive for HIV. I had only been with my husband who was negative.

She smiled bitterly. "It meant I contracted it from a patient without my knowledge, but everyone abandoned me, even my father. I was an only child so had no other siblings to depend on. On my own, I pushed out my baby."

The tears filled her eyes. "Thank God, my baby was born HIV negative, but once that news reached my mother-in-law, she came and took my baby away and I was left on the streets. With the little savings I had I found lodgings in a rundown block, but finding a job I could stomach was much harder, and soon I couldn't even be bothered. That was how I ended up at the soup kitchen for meals.

I get to my feet. "I have one last question. Do you know how his father died?"

"I do," she says, "but it took years for him to finally trust me enough to tell me about it. I'm sorry, darling, but it's not my prerogative to tell his story to anyone else. You'll have to ask him yourself."

I nod and collapse back into the chair.

CHAPTER FIFTEEN

Brand

https://www.youtube.com/watch?v=ou5joAostrw
(Try me)
-oh, take me for a little while-

*I*t is late when I arrive back home from a day full of business meetings. I resolved what others might consider revolting situations, but since I don't suffer from the pangs of conscience other men are burdened with, I had no problems. Once you have torn the liver out of a screaming man, there is not much more that you will not do. Tonight though, I am far from a peaceful mind because far beyond my financial empire and its pesky troubles, is the dark haired, blue eyed, feisty witch under my roof.

I recall our fight last night, the way she lashed out with the knife, and I am suddenly itching for another. Last night I drank myself to sleep, but there is no possibility of going to bed tonight without exorcising this demon. Half out of my mind with exhaustion and lust, I make my way up the stairs. The key is on me. I insert it into the keyhole, and twist the handle open.

She is on her bed and asleep, or perhaps more likely, she is not. I head over to the bottom of the bed and stop to look down on her. The light from the doorway falls on her. She turns then, her hair falling in a dream-like cascade over her eyes and my breath catches in my throat.

It jumpstarts my frustration. How dare she sleep so peacefully? Even the thought of the calm state of her stings all the veins in my body tightly with resentment. I kick the frame of the bed before I can stop myself. The sound startles her awake. Her eyes open wide and for a split second there is confusion in them, but the moment they land on me she instantly jerks up. I circle the bed, watching as she inches back towards the headrest her legs raised to her chin.

I want her terrified, quivering, but her eyes are calm and watchful. It unsettles me to no end. "You offered yourself to me last night ..." I say, allowing a nasty smile to flower on my lips. "I've come to collect."

I wait with bated breath to see what she will do. I watch her glance at the open door and I relish the thought of her jumping off the bed and attempting her escape from the room. Instead she rises to her knees and takes off the tank top she has on.

For the longest time my eyes cannot leave hers. It is like being caught in the most beautiful storm. It is dangerous and yet it is so breathtakingly awesome you cannot run. When I can finally tear my gaze away it slithers down to her full breasts. In the light from the doorway, I can see her nipples are already swollen and nearly as red as her lips, as if someone has been sucking them all night.

My mouth waters.

How is it possible that this sinfully delicious babe has never been fucked by anyone?

Somewhere, there is a stirring of discomfort. A strange sensation. I thought everything in me was dead but the desire for revenge and more material wealth. Suddenly the memories ... oh! the terrible memories come back. Crystal clear, taunting, laughing at me for my weakness. I brought her here to make her suffer not worship her beauty. I rear back. As if she felt the pull back inside me, she lifts her hands and sweeps all of her hair up into a messy mass on top of her head ... and there is no going back for me.

I am so hard for her it hurts.

My trousers come off in an instant and are flung across the room, next is my briefs. Her eyes expand at the size of my exposed cock. It juts towards her, thick and greedy. And the goddess waits in her unbearably provocative pose of capitulation and offering.

Never breaking eye contact I put a knee on the mattress. She draws in a sharp breath. Without warning I pull on her legs so she lands on her back with a gasp of surprise. Stationing her beneath me, I align the length of my body with hers. Her eyes are boring into mine, searching ... but for what I do not know. My heart races feverishly and my mouth suddenly feels parched. She reaches for my shirt. Her fingers tremble as she fumbles with the buttons.

There is too much of a delay so I slap her hands away and crush my mouth to hers. I almost don't want to kiss her, because I can already feel myself losing control, years of discipline slipping and falling in nothing, but I cannot not kiss her. It is like an instinct. The way a baby turns its mouth to its mother's breasts and starts sucking. No one teaches it. It just knows it must do that to survive this harsh world.

The moment I thrust my tongue into her mouth I knew it was a mistake. I'd only intended it to be quick and brutal, just a little taste, but that hard strong thing inside me immediately starts melting, weakening. Even my arms propping me up on either side of her feel as if they are made of warm wax. I have not latched my lips around a life-giving force, I've let my enemy into my heart.

I bruise her lips with the fervent kiss, and I tell myself, I will hurt her as much as she hurts me. The moment her hands come around my neck, I lose all my strength and my body slams on top of her.

Her touch ...

I can feel myself tremble as she splays her fingers over my skin, leaving a burning warmth in its wake. Excitement like I have never known wreaks havoc inside me. I drink in her taste one more time and pull myself away with super human restraint, the growl erupting from my lips is a reflection of the crazy sensations inside me.

I gaze into her eyes, my heart pounding hard. "Go on," I dare her. "Do it. Finish the job. Kill me and you will be free to go back to your father."

Her chest rises and falls as rapidly as mine, her cheeks are flushed a bright red, her mouth swollen from my assault and her eyes, deep unending pools that foretold my doom nine years ago. Even then I knew I was looking straight at what had the ability to imprison my soul.

Her hand tightens, her fingers press on my Adam's apple. I feel the air become constricted. The cells in my body begin to scream for oxygen. I know she is waiting for me to push her hands away. That would be victory for her. My eyes begin to bulge. My cock is still rock hard, but I feel something in the base of my spine begin to flutter uncontrollably. I have to fight every cell, every instinct for survival inside my body not to knock her hands away.

But I do. She will not win. I know she does not have the guts to kill me. Killing me will be like killing herself. For we are one. Tears fill her eyes. With a sob she releases my neck, and waves of pleasure rush through my body as I take large gasping gulps of air. She just watches me with a mixture of horror and shock in her eyes. She thinks she has hurt me, but she has just given me the best victory of my life.

She reaches up to kiss me once again but I hold onto her shoulders and pin her back to the mattress. A kiss is too intimate … No more of that. I'm not ready to fall any deeper into her trap.

"I need my dick serviced, not my heart," I snarl.

Reaching for her round breasts, I grab the full mounds in my hands. She winces at my rough touch, but then bites down on her bottom lip in such a sexy way, I become convinced that her goal is to drive me mad.

Lowering my head, I suck hard on her nipple, and enjoy the pull along my dick. Her moan, soft and like a charm brings an odd sensation of tenderness in my heart. I release the hard bud of one breast and move to the other. I lick, suck, and tug while her nails leave scratches across my back as she gyrates her hips against my cock.

Moving from her breasts I trace kisses down the soft white

skin of her belly. I rip away her panties the moment I arrive at her hips. She immediately closes her thighs like an insect eating flower, trapping my head between her legs. With a smile, I slide a hand up to her chest to hold her down and take her sweet clit in my mouth. It sends a thick trickle of her juice flowing from her opening. When I lap it all up with one hard swipe of my tongue, she almost shoots off the bed.

"Brand," she cries hoarsely.

I press her back down. Fuck, I can't get enough of the taste of this woman. I dip my tongue even deeper into her, then pull it out to smack it hard against the lips of her virgin cunt. My fingers soon join in the assault, sliding in and out of her, while my tongue teases her clit.

All she can do is writhe like a cut snake and emit unintelligent animal sounds.

I lift my head to watch her. I want to see what I'm doing to her. Panting, disoriented, her eyelids half-closed, and her fingers tangled in her hair, she is a hot mess. Her hands shoot out, grab me, and pull me to her. I let myself be pulled up and down on her, her hips grind desperately against my dick. I take my shaft in my hands and slide it up and down her soaking folds. Positioning the tip at her entrance I start to force myself into her. Her eyes widen and she makes a strangled sound at her very first taste of the carnal copulation between a man and a woman.

I am big and she is extremely small and tight.

At her wince of pain, I almost pull out until I remember that my mission is not to give her pleasure. Even so for reasons I care not to think about I cannot bring myself to hurt her at that moment. I restrain myself as much as I can and telling her to relax, I slowly, very slowly, inch by inch make my way into her.

Until I am balls deep in her body.

It is unbelievable, but I'm finally, finally inside Liliana Eden. My chest tightens with a feeling of animalistic and savage possession. The walls of her pussy grip my dick as tightly as a fist and I give in to the groan that erupts from me. Savoring every bit of the achingly sweet pleasure I begin to thrust my hips. Slowly at first, then faster and faster.

She gasps at the tumult of lust that zaps though her body. Strangely, even I feel as though it is my first time. I keep on increasing my speed until my hips are near ramming her off the bed. Meeting my frenzied thrusts, she buckles in for the ride, her hands tightly wrapped around my shoulders as she directs her incoherent cries towards the ceiling.

"Brand ... fu ... fuck. Oh ... f-ffuu ... fuckkk ... Brand ..."

The call of my name has never sounded so sweet. I stare at her, fascinated by the passion of the woman in my arms. She is like a dream that turned into a nightmare, then back to a dream. Soon her whole body begins to quiver. She is about to explode and for some completely inexplicable reason, which has never happened to me before, I want to come with her.

Desperate to do so with her, I forego rhythm and fuck her like a ferocious beast. Her orgasm sets off mine as we roar out together at the fireworks of uncontainable lust. Every vein in my body juts against my skin as the throes of raw, primal sex course through my entire being.

I do not know how long it takes for us both to return to sanity, but when we do, I open my eyes to meet hers. Her pupils are so dilated her irises are almost black. Our faces are so close to one another I am breathing her in and she is breathing me.

I realize with a sense of almost panic that I am holding tightly to her as if my life depended on it, or I care about her, which obviously, I don't. I just lust for her body. Before I can let go she throws her arms around me and captures my mouth in a deep kiss. The taste of her completely undoes me. I want to fuck her all over again, but I know I can't. I'm too exhausted by the emotions she aroused inside me. I roll away from her with the intention of leaving instantly. I need to think, but she grabs my wrist. I look down at her.

"Just stay with me for a few seconds, please," she says softly.

I collapse by her side and shut my eyes. I should go. I know I should. She is too dangerous, but a few seconds later, I reach for her and pull her roughly into me, her perfect buttocks cushioned perfectly against my dick.

Just a few minutes, I tell myself.

I fail. My brain shuts down for the night and drags me into a sleep that no demons are able to wake me up from.

At least a solid six to seven hours later I come awake to the morning sun filtering in through the curtains. With the fog of sleep still upon me, I am not sure of where I am, or why I feel so at peace. Something incredibly warm is pressed against me, and it feels so sweet that I look down in wonder at the angel in my arms. The moment the angel registers as my greatest enemy, I immediately jump up in horror.

My movement is so sudden I send the lamp on the bedside table crashing to the ground, which jerks her awake. Disoriented by the sudden commotion she looks at me curiously.

Furious with myself, I spring off the bed. What the fuck am I doing?

"Are you okay?" she asks, rubbing the sleep away from her eyes.

I don't respond. I don't even bother to pick up my clothes. I just turn around and stomp butt-naked out of the room.

CHAPTER SIXTEEN

Brand

I wake up suddenly, the dream breaking around me.

"Ma," I whisper in the darkness, before I realize the astonishingly vivid images were only an echo from the past.

It was Ma, slathering homemade mayonnaise on her hair to make it shiny and thick, and Da was teasing her about it. Telling her he wouldn't mind the smell so much if it could make her grow a couple of inches taller. My mother was tiny, five feet two inches tall so my father, who well over six feet, took great delight in teasing her about her height. He was also finding new nicknames for her: Little Ant, Shortcake, Midge, Ankle biter. The list was long and colorful.

I get out of bed and pace the floor. Restless. It's been a long time since I dreamed of Ma. Now in the darkness, memories of her tumble into my head. I've made myself forget a great deal of the past, but never her eyes.

They were unforgettable.

Dark, long, and filled with mystery; the eyes of a sorcerer. Probably because she was one. Ma read the tea leaves and cards. Da and me would come home from some gig, and other women from the compound would be leaving our caravan. In her hand Ma would be clutching a five or a ten-pound note, a smile for Da and me, tugging at her lips.

Once when I was still very young I asked her to do a reading for me. She smiled sadly and explained that she had spent her whole life reading the fortunes of many people. More often than not, she had to lie to people about what she saw, because there was always more bad than good in their path. She said she loved me too much to consult the heartless cards for me. She couldn't bear it if she saw something bad.

Sometimes I wondered if that gentle creature ever read her own leaves. If she knew how she would meet her maker, but decided out of the kindness of her heart not to tell us? If she knew her last words would be, "Don't." Or that she would fall dead on the very floor of the kitchen she had spent the afternoon on her hands and knees cleaning. Then I think, no, if she had known she never would have wasted her afternoon in that way. Or maybe, knowing her, she did know, but in death as in life she wanted her body to fall on a clean surface.

The old guilt eats away mercilessly at me.

I hold my head in my hands. God, the past is still so alive in my head. It is ugly and no matter how hard I try I can't get away from it. Three years ago, as I was about to enter a restaurant an old gypsy woman on the sidewalk grabbed my hand. "Buy a flower from me. For good luck," she crowed. I wanted to push her grubby hand away, but I was mesmerized. It was like looking into my mother's eyes again. I pushed a couple of hundred pound notes towards her. She held out the flower. "You become the thing you fight," she warned. I didn't take the flower. But she was right. I've fought with the past for so long it now lives inside me.

I walk to the window and look out into the darkness. The image of Liliana comes into my mind. I think of the uncontrollable way my body reacts to her, and the way I fell so peacefully asleep in her arms. It was the best night I can remember having. I remember the way she had broken apart under me. She didn't hold back. She welcomed me into her body and let me have it all.

She loved it.

But the plan was to torture her as I fucked her. To make her as miserable as I am. And for her to hate every moment of her punishment, and even for myself. I didn't want to get anything out of it but the satisfaction of revenge. The ability to know it is done and walk away a free man. Leave the past behind. Instead, we found indescribable bliss in each other's bodies. In those moments it renders my years of hatred completely pointless.

CHAPTER SEVENTEEN

Brand

I walk into the house just a little past midnight to the sound of laughter. It startles me so much I instantly freeze on the spot. I have never heard laughter in this house before. The voices keep speaking and I immediately recognize them to be Lindy and Liliana.

What the fuck?

With a frown I head towards the kitchen and push open the door. The sight that greets me is one of such domestic bliss that it steals my breath away. If only such a thing was truly possible for me. I have interrupted Liliana and Lindy while they are busy decorating a cake.

My eyes zero in on Liliana. She is wearing one of Lindy's aprons, her cheeks are pink with the heat from the oven, and there is flour or icing sugar on one of them. Her mouth is as red as the strawberries they are using to decorate the frosted cake. At the chill in my eyes the smile disappears from her face.

"Brand," Lindy calls, and I am forced to drag my gaze away from Liliana's.

She smiles uncertainly. "I've made Lancashire hotpot and added extra peppers for you."

"Thank you." I turn towards Liliana again and my voice immediately hardens. "Can I see you for a moment in my study?"

Liliana and Lindy exchange a look before Liliana wipes her hand on a cloth, removes her apron and puts it on the counter, before walking up to me. Shit, she is wearing one of the dresses I ordered for her and the way her hot curves fill it make my eyes water.

I hold the door open for her and she goes through it. We walk in silence down empty corridors. I want to look at her, but I don't let myself. I open my study door and I see her swallow before she walks into the lion's den. I close the door and lean against it. I watch her buttocks move through the thin material of her dress as she walks on ahead.

She stops in the middle of the room, turns towards me and gazes directly into my eyes, and even though she is trying to act confident, I can see uncertainty in her face. She doesn't know what I want or how she should act.

A weird thing happens at that moment, I suddenly realize that I am afraid of her. Of her power over me. And that infuriates me. I am the powerful one here, not her. She is my prey. I can do anything I want to her. I can make her suck my cock right now if I so desire it.

"What have I done wrong now?" she asks quietly. She is calm, but I am not. This is not at all how I planned it. I am supposed to be the one with all the control and she is the one who is supposed to be helplessly at my mercy.

"How dare you laugh?" I ask furiously.

She blinks in surprise.

"Is this a guest house to you? Do you think you're on vacation? Sitting in the kitchen laughing and joking with my staff."

I see her eyes flash with temper. Good. She should be angry too. Because I fucking am. "Vacation? Are you kidding me?"

"Who fucking let you out of your room?"

She lifts her chin proudly. "Lindy invited me to help her out. If you don't want it to happen then you should speak to her."

All I can think about as I watch her is just how beautiful she is, and it causes my temper to rise even more at my lack of self-control. Our night together comes back, and instantly sends a painful shot of arousal straight to my groin that steals my breath.

"You want to hurt me," she says. "Fine, but first, I need you to finish the story you started. What happened to you and your family after you left my home that day? Tell me about your mother."

My hands clench painfully into fists by my side. There she goes again. Taking the initiative. Who the fuck gave her the impression she could demand anything? She is my prisoner.

She shifts her weight from one leg to the other. "Mrs. Parks told me a bit about—"

"Shut the bloody hell up!" I roar, my heart pounding within my chest. I do not even know when I move but in an instant

I am on her, my hands gripping her waist as I rush her backwards and slam her against the wall behind her.

She cries out at the pain, and her hands pull at my wrist to loosen my hold. She claws at my flesh, and when I refuse to set her free, she strikes a bloody slap across my face. It barely registers.

"You do not have the right to ask me about anything," I say between gritted teeth. "Don't ever dare talk about my mother again. Do you understand me?"

She takes a deep breath and nods.

CHAPTER EIGHTEEN

Brand

9 years ago

https://www.youtube.com/watch?v=rPab0qMd-V4

*M*y father was furious with me in the truck. He kept taking his hand of the steering wheel to take a swipe at my head. I stared straight ahead. I didn't care if he was angry. Liliana Eden was mine. All mine. One day I intended to marry that girl.

"I cannot believe I sired such a dolt. Look at you. Who the feck do ya think ya are? Kissing Jake Eden's daughter. Do you know who he is?"

I didn't say anything. He wouldn't understand.

"I'm talking to you. Answer me, boy."

I turned to face my father. "Yeah, I know he is rich, Da, but I can be rich one day too."

My father got so angry his eyes almost popped out of his

head. The truck swerved and someone blew their horn at him. He hung his head out of his car and turned the air blue with curses. They shot past him in fear.

"He's not rich. He's filthy rich, and he's also a cold-blooded killer."

I stared at my father in a mixture of confusion and suspicion. Was he just saying that because he wanted me to stay away from Mr. Eden's daughter? "You're lying. Mr. Eden is a businessman."

My father sneered. "So now you think you're so grown up you know better than me, eh? Let me tell you, you little upstart. Once that businessman was known as Crystal Jake the ruthless gangster and smuggler. When he was your age he was already tying rocks to men's feet and throwing them into the Thames. All of North London belonged to him for ten years. He was so ferocious no one dared to challenge him. He was gunning for the West too, when he met his woman. He gave it up then and went legit, but a leopard never changes its spots. He would slit your throat without a second thought before he'd let you lay one dirty finger on his daughter. She is his favorite. Do ya get what I'm saying, boy?"

All this was news to me. Jake Eden a gangster? I thought of his eyes, how cold and utterly without emotion they had been when he came to tell my father what I had done to his daughter. I realized my da was not lying, but it didn't change a thing. "I'll take my chances," I insisted stubbornly.

"Jesus fucking Christ. Are you the most pig-headed fool in the universe, or am I talking to a two block of wood held together with one nail here?"

"Da, I'm gonna marry that girl. You'll see."

My father swallowed with rage. One of his hands left the steering wheel and shoots straight for my head. He boxed my ear so hard I heard a ringing in my head. "Any more talk like that I swear I'll kill ya, myself."

I said nothing. Just stared straight ahead. As soon as the truck hit the gravel of the road where our caravan was parked, I opened the door, and jumped out, rolling to break my fall. I could hear my father shouting curses at me. I stood up and dusted myself off. I saw my mother open our caravan door.

"What's going on?" she shouted.

My father parked the truck and made his way towards me. I stood my ground. He grabbed me by the neck and forced me back to our little home.

"What's going on?" Ma asked worriedly.

"This boy of yours went and kissed Jake Eden's eldest daughter." He shook his head with disgust. "Better yet, the fool thinks he's got a shot at making her his bride."

Ma's eyes widened with astonishment. She quickly took a step backwards to let us come into the caravan. Her smooth forehead was creased with frown lines. The caravan always felt too small with both my da and me in it, but today it seemed even more cramped. I felt like breaking a window, or running away and not coming back until I had achieved my goal of making Liliana Eden mine.

My father released my neck and looked at me sternly. His black eyes shot sparks of anger. I know he was trying to protect me, but it was not necessary. I had it all worked out. I could take care of myself. I would get a proper job, I would save and when I had enough, I would run away with Liliana.

No one would be able to find us. We'd just be happy together, then when she became heavy with child, her father would have no choice but to forgive us and accept us into his family.

"Is this true?" Ma asked softly.

"Yes," I shouted defiantly. "I love her and I'm gonna marry her, Ma."

My mother stepped forward, both her hands clasped together, "Oh, Brand darling, you can't marry the Eden girl. She's not like us. We're poor folk, definitely not good enough for the likes of her family. Her father will never allow it."

"Yes, tell this blind fool how it is." He turned towards me, his face sneering. "Anyway, I don't know how you plan to marry her, when she doesn't even like you. Tell your ma what she did when you kissed her?"

Ma's eyes widened with surprise and bewilderment, but she turned to Da and defended me loyally. "Can you give your boy a break? He's just a kid. He doesn't understand. Surely you know what first love feels like."

"First love?" my father jeered. "A fecking disgrace is what it is."

I clenched my jaw. He would never understand. No one would. Not even Ma.

My father started laughing cruelly. "What's the matter? Where's all your big talk now, you big stupid wildebeest, eh?"

"Is someone going to tell me what happened?" Ma asked.

"This fool kissed and she ran off crying to her da. He rushed over to me, his face like thunder, and told me to take my son and feck off his land. And never come back." He shook his head regretfully. "The shame. That was a good job too. Jake Eden always paid well."

"I can go and talk to him," I said proudly. "I can tell him that you're not responsible for my actions."

"Oh, listen to him, Ma. Little upstart thinks he's a big man now." He turned to me, and for the first time I saw that he was truly furious. "You dare step one foot on that man's land again and I'll cut it off with my own damn saw. The shame of it. I swear it, Brand, you won't bring shame to this family by going there and begging for any crumbs off his table. You'll forget you ever saw that girl, you hear me, boy?"

"No," I said clearly.

"What did you say?" he bellowed

"I won't forget her, Da. I'm gonna marry her."

My father lunged towards me to hit me, and at the same time my mother ran in front of me, yelling "Don't."

My father's blow caught her on the side of her forehead. It should have been nothing. If it had reached me, it would have hurt less than the one he gave me in the truck, but the force of his blow made my tiny mother fly into the air. Her scream started and ended when she hit her head on the edge of the stove. Then she fell face down on the kitchen floor. And remained unmoving.

For a few seconds neither my father or me moved. We were too stunned. Too amazed to comprehend the situation. Then my father staggered forward and fell next to her. He turned her over. There was no blood, no real indication that it was serious. He stroked her face, he touched her closed eyelids, he kissed her unresponsive lips again and again. He called her name, he shook her, he cried, he howled, but she never woke up again.

Her neck was broken high up on her spinal column. Later I would find out that the freak accident had caused an internal decapitation.

In that one crazy instant, she went away from us. Forever.

CHAPTER NINETEEN

Liliana

*A*t my silent nod, Brand lets go of me. Any arousal I saw when I first came into the room is gone from his cold black eyes. He looks down at me with disgust.

"Take your clothes off. I want to fuck you again."

I know what he is doing. He is trying to humiliate me, but I won't let him. Brand Vaughan is not going to intimidate me any further. I am certain that he is unwilling to kill me, at least for now, so I have to do my best to stand up to him, and find a way to resolve his grudge. This might be the only way I walk out of this nightmare. I lick my dry lips. "Yes, we can … do it again, if you want, but we have to use condoms from now on."

His eyes fill with real amusement. It makes him look even more attractive. "I went in bare the last time … and I think I liked that very fucking much."

I square my shoulders. "I don't want to get pregnant."

"Bit late to be worrying about that, don't you think? You might already be carrying my bastard child."

"I took a morning after pill after the last time. I asked Mrs. Parks to get it for me."

He cocks his head and contemplates me. "Mmm ... it's an interesting idea to see your belly growing big with my seed. It will be the perfect punishment. You'll stay with me until you give birth, and then I'll keep the child and send you back to your da."

"I'd rather die than bring a child into this world so it can suffer with a monster like you. We had an agreement. You can have my body, but not children."

He laughs mockingly. "My, my, it was actually a repugnant idea, but the more you reveal how much you hate the thought the more attractive it becomes."

"This is non-negotiable. I don't think a child should be conceived in such an ire of hatred."

"Actually, I agree with you. You can have your bloody condoms."

I exhale with sheer relief. "Thank you. There is one more thing."

He raises an enquiring eyebrow.

"I need to speak to my mother. She is very delicate, and I want to talk to her and reassure her that I'm fine." My words were rushed in my eagerness to impress upon him how important it is that I am allowed to speak to her.

His eyes show no emotion. "There you go again making all kinds of demands. Spoilt little Liliana. Give her an inch and she wants a mile."

I panic. I never thought he would say no to this request. "Please. I won't ask for anything else. I just want to reassure my poor mother."

"No," he says shortly.

I stare at him in horror. "Why? Why do you have to hurt her? She has never done anything to you."

"Because it hurts you when I hurt her."

In that moment I forget everything Mrs. Parks told me. Any feeling of pity or empathy is gone, and I wonder how it is possible for anyone to hate another human being so much. I forget about being calm and negotiating and just lash out. "You're so angry with the whole world because you had to suffer, but the problem is not the world. It is *you*. You are the problem. YOU. *You* are a selfish pig who thinks the whole world owes you something. So I ran and told my father about the kiss, and I'm really sorry something bad happened to your family as a result, but that's just life. Bad things happen. Other people get over it. Maybe you should try it instead of living inside all this fake drama."

I know I have touched a nerve because his eyes glitter with fury. His fingers dig brutally into the flesh of my arm as he drags me along. I am literally pushed into my room and the door bangs shut behind me. I totter and fall to the ground. The sound of the lock is loud. Then I hear him speak on his cellphone and the words he says shock me so much I freeze.

"Send me Eden's location," he snaps.

Fear grips my heart. Jesus Christ, what have I done? What is he going to do? The fear threatens to suffocate me. I rush to the door and bang on it, calling for him, calling for Mrs. Parks, but I know that it is fruitless. He won't open the door, and she won't be able to hear me. Even if she does she will be too conflicted by her loyalty to the monster who has become her son, to answer.

The door is a solid oak monstrosity, and at least a century old: thick, and impervious, it almost drives me to madness with frustration, but still, I cannot stop. I cannot give up. I have to do everything I can to help my dad. I continue to pound on the door, my legs flailing out to kick at it violently until my knuckles are bleeding and my foot swollen from the kicks. Only when my toe is finally injured that I limp away to settle back on the floor.

*T*he stubbed toe in one hand and close to tears, I angrily brush my hair out of my eyes.

I'd hoped having sex with me would ease his anger and soften him towards me, but it now seems as if it has only fired up the force of his vendetta against me.

My mind goes back to the time I offered myself to him … when he took me to a place that I'd never been. It was as though I was possessed. Or a different person. I had expected that the intensity of our passion together would make a difference, but this evening showed me nothing had changed. He *hated* me.

With a sob, I bury my head between my knees. My nails dig into my fisted hands.

Oh Daddy, I'm so very, very sorry I didn't keep my cool. I'm so sorry I told you about the stupid kiss.

As soon as I get home I go to the kitchen. I find my baby staring out of the window. She turns to look at me. I walk up to her, my arms open and she walks into them. I bend my head to inhale the scent of her hair, and my entire body tenses with shock. She has been using Liliana's shampoo.

"Oh, baby," I whisper and crush her to me. I feel so fucking helpless. For a few seconds neither of us move. I let the feeling of her flesh pressed into mine wash away the tiredness from my bones.

Then she tilts her head up. "Shall I make some food for you?"

I shake my head. "No, I'm not hungry."

She frowns. "When was the last time you ate?"

"I ... er ... lunch."

"Today?"

"Yesterday."

"Oh, darling. You have to eat. She needs both of us to be at our best."

"Yeah," I say softly. Where the fuck are you, Liliana?

"So Shane's tip didn't work out," she says sadly.

"No, it was someone else's daughter."

"I bet her parents were very happy to get their daughter back."

"I guess so. One of the guys took her back."

She sighs heavily. "What do we do now, Jake?"

"We keep looking. I won't stop until I find her."

"Do you think she'll call again?"

"If I know her, she'll try her damndest. Just be patient. Everything is hooked up. All you have to do is keep her on the phone for as long as you can. Keep talking. Don't ask her questions about where she is or anything that will cause her captors to cut off the call. Talk about her sisters, how her dog is doing, how sorry I am for messing up her job. Inane things. As if we truly believe that she has gone to Spain because she is angry with me. We have one chance."

She nods vigorously. "I've already practiced everything I will say." She reaches into her jeans pocket and pulls out a folded piece of paper. "I've even got it all written down in note form so I don't mess up and say the wrong thing."

"Good girl," I say with a smile.

She nods again. "We'll find her, Jake. You'll find her. No one can outsmart you for long." Suddenly tears start filling her eyes. "They took my baby. I've already lost one. I just can't lose another one."

I pull her body against mine and hold her tightly. "We will find her."

"I keep wondering why they have taken her. There has been no demand for money. What could it be? And they allowed her to call us. So it can't even be human trafficking."

I stroke her hair. "It's me. This is about me."

She presses her lips together. She is not stupid. She has already figured that out. She just didn't want it to be true.

A bleep makes both of us freeze. Immediately, I pull my phone out of my jacket and look at the message.

Want her back? Come to Sturminster,
train station platform to London. 7.00pm today.
Don't be late and come alone.

*L*ily's eyes are huge. "You're not going alone, are you?"

I nod decisively. "Yes, I am. If he knows this number, then he knows a lot about us. I can't afford to take the chance he will not follow me to that address."

She frowns. "That's really strange. He knows all about you. Right down to this ex-directory phone number. Why didn't he tell you not to come armed?"

She has a point. Something is not right, but I'm going anyway. If it is my life he wants in exchange for Liliana's then so be it.

CHAPTER TWENTY-ONE
Brand

*M*ark is by my side as I hunker down on the pedal of my BMW, our speed moving dangerously past a hundred and thirty miles an hour. I can see him sneaking concerned looks at me.

"Are you certain he is still on M3?" I ask, my gaze razor-sharp and focused on the road.

He looks down to his phone to catch the tracker on it. "He is, but he is heading towards Junction Eight now. I think he's going to take the A303 exit to Salisbury."

Good, he is on his way to Sturminster. This is good. This is very good. The worry over his daughter has made him careless. He would never have made this trip on his own otherwise. I head down the exit and increase my speed on the dark road. The moment I spot the Lamborghini Urus ahead of me I know it is him even before Mark makes the connection. Not that I need the confirmation as the name EDEN is written boldly across his plate. The arrogant bastard.

"That's him right there," Mark says, a note of reverence in his voice. After all these years he is still an awe-inspiring figure in the underworld.

There are only a few cars on the road, and I step on the gas, the engine revving to its limit as we fly into the night towards catastrophe, the trees on both sides zooming past like ghosts.

"Boss ..." Mark shouts out in fear.

"Put on your bloody seat belt and shut the fuck up," I snarl.

He sits upright and buckles in for a crash. It happens in a flash, and despite Jake Eden's desperate attempt to divert his vehicle from the impending collision, my SUV smashes right into the side of his car. It makes his vehicle somersault into the air, as mine spins continuously and endlessly on the highway. Moments away from claiming both of our lives, it comes to a stop just before we crash into an articulated truck.

My car is not badly damaged, but Jake Eden's car on the other hand has been flung into the woods. Mark is moaning quietly. I unbuckle my belt quickly and get out. As I hear the hiss and poof of the dented bonnet, I feel something trickling down the side of my face.

I know it is blood, but I couldn't care less. Swiping my hand across the wound and wiping the blood on my coat, I head into the woods in search of him.

I find the Urus upside down and damaged even more than my car.

I look through the window and see Jake Eden unconscious inside. A strange thrill of excitement flows through my body. This is it. This is the moment I take my revenge. It's either him or me.

When I try the door, it is either jammed or locked. Breaking the window, I put my hand inside and start to jerk the door open. It is a feat, but eventually it budges and swings open. For a moment and with the light from the streetlamps, I stop to watch him. It has been almost a decade since I was last so close to the swine who drove my father to his death. I pull him out of the driver's seat and drop him on the ground.

Mark is holding his head and hurrying over to me. "Is he alive?"

"Yeah," I say, staring down at my greatest enemy, the man I hate with every cell in my body.

"The police will be here soon," Mark said worriedly behind me.

"Pass me your knife," I say without turning to look at Mark.

Without a word he produces the glistening steel and hands it over.

CHAPTER TWENTY-TWO

Brand

9 years ago

https://www.youtube.com/watch?v=A9hcJgtnm6Q
-nothing, nothing, nothing gonna save us now-

*M*y father yelled so loudly the entire caravan shook. I'd never seen him that way and even more than her death—which shock had not allowed my brain to properly register yet—his reaction terrified me. His eyes were blood shot and the pain so etched into the lines in his face that I almost could not recognize him. But more than sorrow he was furious. Inconsolably furious because she had gone so suddenly.

"Come back!" He shook her lifeless body mercilessly. "Come back and leave properly, you selfish little bitch. Come the feck back. Whitney Vaughan come the feck back, right now!"

He swore that he would never forgive her. Then I stood there staring at him blankly as he began to shatter everything around. I was afraid for my father. I was afraid he was going to hurt himself. I was afraid he had gone mad. He was banging his head against a wall and his hands were bleeding from breaking the glass cabinet where my mother stored all her precious red crystal. He had broken every single piece. Every time he broke one he called her to come back and stop him. The inhabitants of the other caravans had started to gather around our door. They did not come in. They knew better, but I could see their shadows outside the curtains.

"Da—" I began, but he rushed at me and struck such a blow across my face I was flung halfway across the caravan. I crashed against the toilet door. Never in my life had I felt such a pain and for the longest of time I couldn't even move. All I could do was feel, the deadly pain of what I was sure was a broken jaw, and its reverberation through my entire body. I was shaking as I tried to breathe, tears beginning to well up in my eyes.

"It's you. It's your fault. You killed her. If not for you none of this would have happened," he roared, his face purple with uncontrollable rage.

Outside, someone began to knock on the door.

"Fuck off," my father bellowed, whirling around like a dervish. Truly he had gone insane with grief. He grabbed a kitchen knife and began to wield it, slashing the empty air, screaming. Telling the people gathered outside that he would kill them if they entered.

Gypsies never call the police. They hate us and we refuse to give our faith or respect to them. So we would never willingly give them a foothold into our lives. No matter what our troubles, we solve them ourselves.

The men outside began to try to reason with my father, but the more they tried, the angrier and more out of control he became. Then, one of the oldest women in our community, a frightening hag, was called. She screeched out to my da that my mother was outside the door and calling to him. My father stopped in his tracks and ran out of the door. The men outside pounced on him and sat on him. It took six men to hold him down. When he would not calm down they punched his lights out.

When my father came around a few hours later he was a different person. He asked for my mother, but when one of the men told him she was gone, he gazed up at me. Stubble shadowed his cheeks and jaw, and his eyes were sunken and blank. He looked utterly haggard. It was an astounding contrast from the man he had been a few hours ago.

"Da," I called, but he shook his head and sat up slowly.

He looked around him. "Where is she?"

"She is on the bed," I whispered.

He got up and went to the bedroom and closed the door. For twenty minutes he stayed inside. We could hear him muttering and shuffling around. Then he came out and closed the door behind him. Without even looking at me, he went out of the door and walked towards his truck.

I ran behind him. "Da, where are you going?"

"Never mind that. You take care of your ma," he said opening the car door. He hopped into the driver's seat and closed the door.

"Da," I called.

He turned his face and looked down at me. It was like I was a stranger. I knew then I was dead to him. He blamed me for what happened. If I hadn't insisted on marrying Liliana none of this would have happened. I never saw him alive again.

When I went back into the bedroom, I saw that he had dressed my mother in her favorite blue dress. He had combed her hair and put a tiara in it and tried to put lipstick on her lips, but it was all smudged. I wiped the lipstick away and carefully reapplied it. Her skin was warm, but there was something frighteningly still about her. It made the hairs on my neck stand. I kissed her cheeks. I could smell the faint whiff of mayonnaise from her hair.

It did not seem real. This was just a nightmare. She couldn't be dead. How could she be dead when she was so alive an hour ago? I lay down next to her and listened carefully, but I could not hear her heart beating. It was always so steady. She said she wanted to see my grandchildren. I closed my eyes and held her still hand. My chest felt as if someone was sitting on it.

"Ma," I called as if she would magically come alive if I called her.

She didn't come alive. A few hours later, the flashing blue lights of police cars came onto our site. My father had given himself up at the police station. They took me into the care system. The hellish care system for orphans and vulnerable children.

CHAPTER TWENTY-THREE

Brand

https://www.youtube.com/watch?v=OpQFFLBMEPI

*T*he moment I arrive back at the house, I dash through the front door, and up the stairs. I unlock the door of Liliana's room and throw it open. She is standing by the bed, her feet shoulder-width apart, knees bent, and her face wary and watching.

My heart races as I casually take a seat on one of the armchairs. I pop my feet on the coffee table and smile. "You can sit back down," I drawl. "I know you think I am a self-absorbed jerk, but I have a present for you."

She says nothing, her head is slightly cocked and watches me suspiciously.

"What's the matter? Don't you like presents? Don't you want to know what I got for you?"

She frowns. "What is it?"

Taking my legs off the table, I reach into my jacket and retrieve the ziplock bag. Holding it up in the air, I let it drop down on the table.

At first her eyes narrow in incomprehension, not quite sure of what she is seeing, but when it registers, all the blood drains away from her face. She stares at it as if it were a serpent. "What is it?" she asks as if she cannot believe what she is seeing.

"Oh, I'm sorry," I apologize, "perhaps you need a closer look."

I throw the transparent bag to her and she catches it with both hands. I swear that I can almost feel her heart jump the moment she recognizes what is inside the bag. I lean back again into the chair as she sinks to her knees, unable to hold herself upright any longer. She opens the bag, takes out Jake's lion head ring, and looks at it in disbelief.

Which is weird, because my intention was to bring the ring attached to Jake Eden's middle finger, but as I crouched next to his unconscious body I had hesitated. I looked at him, bloodied and breathing shallowly from the crash, and even then, he was something special. He was that thing that caused men to speak of him as if he was a god or a demon. Even a ruthless killer like him was willing to sacrifice his own life for love. I had no love in my life, but I was entranced by the idea. Love was indeed the most powerful force that exists.

If I took him down this way I would always know I was not better than him. That I had not fought him fair and square. I had done the cowardly thing. I was no coward. I bent down and pulled his ring off and brought it to his daughter as my bargaining chip.

Trembling with fear, and full of disbelief, Liliana looks up at me. Her eyes are completely devastated. "You *bastard,*" she swears. "You're ... y-you're insane."

I accept the endearment wholeheartedly, but a strange discomfort I can't shake off takes hold of my insides. I did not expect such grief from her. It is only his ring. Not his finger. I only wanted to show her I could get to her father and to force her to obey me.

"What have you done to my father?" she demands in a whisper. "This is the ring my mother gave him on their first wedding anniversary, and I have never seen him without it. He would never have given it to you. How did you get it?"

I watch her, the pain in her eyes.

"What did you do to him?"

I sit up suddenly angry with myself. Why am I letting her make me feel bad? What about the years I felt like shit? "I crashed my car into his Urus and it somersaulted into the air, multiple times before finally landing in the woods."

Her jaw drops. "What?"

"For the most part he is going to be fine, one would think so anyway, since he seemed to have hardly any injuries, but he should count himself very lucky. I was going to cut his middle finger off so he won't be able to fuck the world up any more." I lean back into the chair. "Damn, my personality is gold, how can I be so entertaining?"

Liliana charges me suddenly. I see her flying at me and it is quite amusing. It takes less than a medium grip around her arms to break her attack.

"Woah!" I say cheerfully. "You're getting feisty too quickly. I'm not finished with my report."

I push her away, watching as she staggers backwards and falls on her delectable ass.

"I don't know why you are so upset. Surely, this was a long time coming," I ask. "You might not know the details, but you must have suspected the real businesses he ran behind the scenes. The ones that fueled all your father's other companies. No doubt he tried to keep it from you, his little princess, but it would be very disappointing if you were that easily fooled."

She raises her chin. "You're wrong about my father. Yes, circumstances forced him to spend his youth on the wrong side of the law, but he gave it up when he met my mother."

"Awww ... that was his big excuse. Circumstances. Well, I had 'circumstances' too, but I'm not going to hide behind that bullshit. I'm a bastard because I want to be one. It's far more fun."

She drops to her knees then and tears fill her beautiful eyes and run down her face. "Pl-please Brand," she says, her hands pressed together for the plea. "Please don't hurt my father."

"Aha!" I say victoriously. This is exactly what I hoped for. Total subjugation. "I've been waiting for you to get on with your pleas. You are one smart woman."

Rising to my feet, I unbuckle my belt and unzip my trousers. I watch her stare as my cock springs free, thick and already aroused.

I shake my head at it. "I apologize," I say as I stroke along the solid length. "It's been clamoring for you ever since our first night. If it had made sex an ordeal for you like I had intended to, then none of this would have been necessary. Instead it ended up almost making us both lose our minds from the pleasure. Sex between us can be anything but pleasurable. When I fuck you, misery and guilt should be all that either of us feels."

"You are sick" she says, disgusted.

"I know," I murmur. "Pain ... and staggering loss does that to you. You have a glimpse of that now. Crawl towards me, baby ..." My eyes stare intently into hers. "Suck me off ... and I will spare your father."

My gaze taunts her with the challenge. I don't know if I really expected it, but she begins to crawl towards me. My blood brims with anticipation, and my cock juts eagerly towards her as she approaches. But when she reaches me all I can see are her wet eyes.

Unable to stand her gaze for a moment longer I grab her head and pull it forward. The tears keep streaming down her face. I try to force a smile to mine but it is impossible. It is perfect, we are both miserable, but as her mouth shakily covers my cock, I feel only pain.

She has no right to do this to me. I grab her hair. "Suck hard on the head," I instruct harshly. "Slide your tongue down the length and then grip the base with your hand." I tug on her hair to bring her eyes up to mine. "Hard!"

She grabs my cock to do as she has been told, and my eyes flutter and close as an ethereal groan escapes my lips. "Take as much of it into your mouth as you can ... I want to feel my tip all the way at the back of your throat." She pulls my rod into her mouth and begins to suck hard on it. "Hmmm ... just like that." I breathe heavily as I move my hips to thrust it deeper into her mouth, but she doesn't have the experience to deep throat, and she begins to gag and choke. I pull her mouth away and a burst of pre-cum shoots out.

With an iron fist, I finish the job myself, fisting my penis brutally until I reach the point of no return. I explode at the ecstasy and revel in the waves. When I open my eyes she is watching me, her eyes seemingly haunted. I rise to my feet then and instantly she grabs my legs.

"Brand ... please," she begins, "just give me another chance," she cries.

At the look in her eyes brimming with tears, I feel something strike me so hard in the center of my heart that I lightly stagger backwards. The chair breaks my fall but my eyes remain on hers. Before I can stop it, my eyes fill with tears also. She falls to the ground sobbing. I stare at her for a long time. In disbelief. Look at what I have done. I have broken her. Then I pick her up gently off the floor. I carry her to the bed and lay her down gently. When I straighten she is gazing into my eyes. Hers are like crushed flowers.

"Do what you like with me, but please don't hurt my family anymore," she whispers brokenly.

I nod and walk out of her room and lock the door behind me.

CHAPTER TWENTY-FOUR

Liliana

I cry until I'm so drained and exhausted it feels as if I am nothing but an empty husk. I can't stop thinking of my father, and praying that he is okay. Into my misery comes the sound of footsteps. I turn my head towards the door and listen listlessly. I can tell they don't belong to Brand. Probably, a maid with a tray of food. It must be dinner time. Too tired to care I don't move even when a key is inserted into the door, and the handle twists. But when the door is pushed softly open, I summon the energy to sit up.

Mrs. Parks stands at the door and looks at me with eyes full of pity. She is carrying my dinner tray. I notice that she leaves the door open as she heads towards the coffee table to place my dinner there.

She straightens to look at me, and I respond with a silent plea in my eyes.

"You need to eat," she says.

Hot, bitter tears that I could have sworn I'd run out of well up anew in my eyes and roll down my cheeks. I press my father's ring to my chest and her eyes flutter down to it.

"I cannot do anything intentionally against Brand," she says softly. "He didn't come from my body, but he is my *son*."

"Please. You don't have to do anything against him. Just leave the door unlocked."

She frowns. "I can't let you go out there. You'll die out there."

"I'll die in here. I'll take my chances. I'll dress warmly. I grew up in the country and I know how to navigate the wilderness. I know I can make it to the farmhouse. I promise I will never get Brand in trouble. I won't tell anyone about this kidnapping, not even my own family."

She shakes her head, but there is uncertainty in her eyes.

I quickly take advantage of that momentary hesitation. "Please, Mrs. Parks. You have to believe me that I will never get Brand in trouble. I'll leave and that thing that was between us will be over. It will be better for Brand too. This is an unhealthy obsession. When I am gone, he will realize it."

She takes a step towards me as if she wants to comfort me, then she stops herself and heads back to the door. It crosses my mind that if I rush her I can probably overpower her, but I would hate to hurt her. She is a truly kind soul who has been put into a horrible position. For a second she stands at the open doorway then she turns and places her index finger to her lips before putting the key in her pocket.

"Be very careful," she says, and with a sad smile walks away.

For a second I do nothing. Just listen as I swipe the tears off my face, and hurry into the closet. Using my teeth, I nick then tear a dress and turn it into a cap. Quickly I construct a few layers of clothes. Then I grab my jacket and zip myself into it. I break off the high heels on the warmest looking pair of boots and slip my feet into them. I will continue to try and escape until my very last breath.

I sprint out of the room and down the eerily quiet corridor, keeping to the walls like a bug. Somehow I arrive at the kitchen that has been closed down for the night without meeting anyone. I find my way towards the back door. I pull it open and the blast of cold air that bombards me is so icy it actually chills my bones.

Beyond the garden is the infinite darkness of a vast hunting moor. I circle the house until I reach the area where I figured I saw the lights of the farmhouse in the distance. I could see it when I was high up, at ground level I cannot see it. I will have to trust my instincts. Hell, it is freezing cold. I should run. That will keep me warm. If I can just get there. Hopefully someone will be there and I will be able to contact my dad and he will come and get me. I'll have to make up a believable story for him though.

I touch the slight bulge of my father's ring pressed between my bra and my heart. "Wait for me, Dad. I'm bringing your ring back. Then I run out into the darkness.

CHAPTER TWENTY-FIVE

Brand

*I*t has been almost half-an-hour that I have felt restless and strange. The feeling comes from deep inside my gut. At first I tried to ignore it, but as the seconds tick by it is getting worse and worse.

Rising to my feet I begin to walk. I exit the study almost unaware of where I am until I am standing in front of Liliana's door. As I reach for my key I hear quiet footsteps behind me. I glance back and what I see makes me turn around and keep my eyes on her until she stands before me.

"What is it?" I ask, impatience in my voice.

"I left the door open for her," she says quietly.

I couldn't have heard her correctly. My eyebrows furrow in annoyance. "Excuse me?"

"I left the door unlocked," she repeats, her voice defiant.

My blood begins to boil, but I cannot bring myself to chastise her. Not her. I shut my eyes for a moment to contain myself.

When I reopen my eyes she is staring boldly back at me. "You never interfere," I remind her.

"Not this time," she says, lifting her head proudly. "I did what my heart told me to do. Punish me if you must."

I glare at her. She knows just as well as I do that I will do nothing to her. I throw open the door to reveal the predictably empty room. I go very still as I look around the room and see how carefully she has prepared for the long trek out of the moors. I pull out my phone and give quick orders and in no time Mark comes jogging up the stairs. With one look he figures out what has happened and gives me a look filled with dread.

"Get Andrew and Tim here *now*. I want to know what happened in the surveillance room."

He pages Andrew and Tim, then turns to me. "I'll send out Khaled's team for a quick search, Boss." When I don't respond, he goes on. "We will find her. There is no way she could have got far on foot."

"Do you realize it's minus two degrees out there?" I ask quietly. I am insanely calm. Usually, my temper is hair trigger and at the least provocation I will blow a gasket and unleash hell on everyone around me. I don't know why I am calm. I might be in shock. I can't believe she slipped through my fingers.

Mark looks at me strangely as if he can't quite believe his eyes. He is saved from answering my rhetorical question when Andrew and Tim come barreling into the room. I turn towards them as they stand there, their mouths slightly agape as they pant.

"Where were you both?" I demand.

"Mrs. Parks invited us for Lancashire Hotpot," Tim mutters defensively, his eyes sliding to the ground.

I instantly understand what happened. "Go on. Get out of here all of you and find her," I order, "or there'll be hell to pay."

"I'll go too, and see what I can do," Mark mumbles uncomfortably and exits the room after them. I exhale slowly. Then I lift my hand and smash my fist on the coffee table. It cracks with a loud noise as white pain shoots up my arm. I am glad for the throbbing injury. My little bird flew away. If anything at all has happened to her ...

"I'm sorry," Mrs. Park whispers. "She said she had grown up in the country and knew how to take care of herself."

I take a deep breath and turn to face the window. It has started snowing. My mind feels crystal clear. It is a good thing. It means the temperature has gone up to zero degrees and she will start leaving tracks. Also the snow is falling fast and deep and the roads will soon become unpassable, so no one will be able to take her out to the village.

Running down the stairs I snatch my coat from the rack and sprint out of the house leaving the front door wide open. I can see the tracks my men have left as they scattered in different directions. I run around the side of the house as soon as I reach the area that is almost a straight path to the farmhouse. I start running towards it while letting my eyes sweep either side of me. I do not use the torch on my phone because I know if I do my eyes will only see inside the narrow band of its light. This way my eyes will slowly train themselves to see in the dark. The farmhouse is actually a lot further away than it looks from the house.

I run to the edge of my land and see nothing at all. No bits of clothing caught in brambles. Only a flat white landscape. Its beauty hides an uncaring heart. I stop to think. All her tracks have been covered by the snow, and I have not yet reached any fresh tracks. I know I am going in the right direction, but what if she got lost in the dark? I stop and rethink my strategy. I run to the stables and saddle Ramses. He is a shining black beauty. It was Jake Eden who got me interested in horses. He was such an impressive horseman. I wanted to be better than him.

"Let's go," I say, and Ramses takes off into the night as if on wings.

Cold air rushes past my ears. My plan is to move in a criss-cross movement towards the farmhouse. That way even if she went off course, I'll find her. Hot vapor billows out of Ramses's nostrils as he thunders over the hard ground. I pull on the reins hard and he comes to a juddering stop. I jump off him. A wisp of cloth sticking out of the snow. I fish it out. There is fresh blood on it. The horror is indescribable. I leap back on the saddle and keep my pace steady as I work my way over the land. Then I see it. The small dark shape on the ground.

I dig my heels in and make for it. My heart feels like it is going to burst out of my chest. She is lying face up and not moving. Snow has started to lay even on her face. I slide off Ramses and crouch next to her. Jesus, her lips are already turning blue.

She is as still as death as I run my hands down her face then her body. I find the source of the blood quickly. A tear in her arm. Not serious. The blood is already clotting. I press my fingers to her pulse. It is faint, but it is there. Inside me something collapses from sheer relief. Under her head I find a swelling as big as a pigeon's egg. She must have fallen and knocked herself out. I take off my jacket and wrap it around her frame.

I lift her into my arms, and as gently as I can lay her over Ramses. In the distance I can see the men's torchlights going further away from the house. Big flakes of snow fall steadily on us as I get on the horse and carefully transfer her into my arms. She doesn't make a sound and that terrifies me.

I turn Ramses towards the house and prompt him to a gallop. I am in a race against my entire world collapsing at my very feet. As my trusty stallion flies us home I feel hot blinding tears fill my eyes. They roll down my face and I am powerless to stop them.

CHAPTER TWENTY-SIX

Liliana

I awaken in an unfamiliar room.

Over my face is an oxygen mask, and as I turn my head slowly to the side I see that an IV drip has been attached to my arm and I'm wearing what looks like a hospital gown. My mind feels foggy, and it takes a few moments for me to recall with decent clarity what happened.

Yes, I was running away.

To look for my father. All I could think about was him even as I became colder and colder and began to lose my sense of direction in the pitch black. I could have been running in circles. The lights of the farmhouse that I had been so sure was in the direction I was travelling in never materialized. I recall stumbling on a piece of jutting rock and falling, crying out 'Daddy' at the sharp excruciating pain at the back of my head ... then the world faded into blessed blackness.

Does this mean I was rescued?

Some part of me cries out with sorrow at the thought, but

another part of me galvanizes into action. I need to get to my dad. With my good hand I remove the mask from my face. The grief I feel gives me some sort of strength to sit up. It is then that I hear the low sound of the television on, and the mention of my family's name. I turn to it and with widened eyes begin to watch the report of my father's accident. Blinking my tears away I listen even more closely and almost collapse back in relief when I see that he is all right.

I need no further motivation. I pull the IV out and holding onto the bed, I try to stand, but there is no strength in my legs and my body feels as heavy as lead. Letting my body drop to the floor, I crawl towards the wall, lift myself up, and lean against it.

With the wall as my support, I take careful steps out of the room.

It must be the dead of night because the corridor is completely empty of staff or patients. I'd hoped to meet someone who I could have begged to take a message for me, but never mind. My legs were already feeling a lot stronger and I just had to keep going until I could find a door or elevator. After what seems like a lifetime I reach a set of elevator doors. I press the button and, barely able to breathe, wait for it.

It dings open and my gaze clashes with Brand's chilling eyes. He looks as if he's just seen a ghost and I'm so startled I lose the careful concentration that had kept me up and I fall backwards, landing on my butt. Jarring pain comes from everywhere. I feel broken in a thousand different ways.

"Jesus Christ," he growls, taking a step towards me.

I begin to crawl backwards on my hands. I open my mouth to tell him to stay away, but I am barely able to sound the words.

His polished black shoes stop next to me. I freeze. Crouching down, he hooks his hands under my knees and my back and scoops me into his strong arms. Silently, he carries me back through the corridor I'd just come through. I try not let my head rest against his chest even though every nerve ending in my body is begging me to.

"We are not in a hospital?" I whisper.

He frowns. "No. Why would you think that?"

"Why don't you let me go, Brand?" I ask restlessly. My skin feels hot and feverish and I can't look him in the eye.

He ignores my question.

"That's the best way for you to stay alive," I ramble on. "If you keep me here much longer my father will find me, then there will truly be nowhere for you to hide."

He smiles cruelly. "How amusing? You think I should fear that old, toothless lion. He has been out of the business for twenty years now. This turf is mine. I am the new king. I have just as much power if not more than he wielded in his heyday."

He enters the room where I had woken up and I say. "You can put me down here. I need to go to the toilet."

Instead of setting me on the ground he carries me into the bathroom. Gently he seats me on the toilet.

"You can go now. I can manage on my own," I say tightly.

"The time for modesty is past," he mocks.

"I can't do it with you watching," I lash angrily.

He sighs and turns his back.

"After I have emptied my bladder, he runs a washcloth under the tap. Then he crouches next to me and to my complete shock he wipes me gently with the warm washcloth.

"Why are you doing this? You've already had me. Your revenge is complete. Why do you want me here when you hate me?"

He dumps the washcloth in the basin and lifts me into his arms again. Walking over to the bed, he lays me down on it and tenderly strokes my hair. I look into his face in astonishment. The expression on his face is one of softness. Then he lets his hand slide down my body and lifts up my gown exposing my sex. With both his hands he pushes my thighs apart.

I start to shiver at the expression in his eyes. Even in the state I am in, I feel my body respond to his. I can feel myself becoming wet. He bends his dark head and swipes his tongue along my slit and my treacherous body arches with pleasure.

He brings his gaze back up to my face. "Yes, I do hate you, Liliana Eden, but I am like a heroin addict. I need my poison. I'll do anything, even kill for it."

We stare at each other for what seems like an eternity. Then he puts his mouth back on my pussy and does not lift his head until my hands are clawing through his hair and I break into a million drops on his tongue. Afterwards he pulls my gown back down, and turns to go, but I grab his wrist. His eyes find mine, his are black and veiled.

"It's my birthday tomorrow and I would like to speak to my father. Please."

For a few heart-stopping seconds he just stares at me, an expression I cannot decipher in his eyes, then he nods. "All right. Mark will set up the necessary equipment so you can speak to him on an untraceable connection."

Even before I can thank him, he has turned and walked away. I listen to the sound his polished black shoes make on the corridor outside until there is silence again. Alone I contemplate my little victory and what I can tell Dad that will not terrify him. Less than five minutes later there are footsteps outside again. They are not his and my body tightens with fear. The door opens and a bespectacled, round man in a doctor's coat enters.

He tuts. "You've pulled your IV off." He comes to the edge of the bed and starts to take my vitals without introducing himself. "Never mind it was just a precaution." He smiles benignly. "Looks like you are on the mend. I suppose you have a headache?"

I shake my head.

"That's good. If you have any pains I could prescribe some painkillers?"

I know I definitely don't want to take any drugs from a doctor who is in the employ of a criminal. "I don't have any pain," I say in a clear voice.

"Fine. Are you hungry?"

My stomach growls and he laughs. "I'll send someone in with food for you.

CHAPTER TWENTY-SEVEN

Liliana

*N*ot long after the doctor leaves, the door is pulled open by Mrs. Parks. She comes in with a tray. With her face full of worry she hurries over to take the seat by my side.

"How are you feeling?" she asks softly.

"I'm okay," I say, picking at the bed linen with my fingers.

Her sigh is heavy with regret. "If I had known this would happen I wouldn't have allowed you to leave. I didn't properly think it through. I put your life in danger and I'm sorry."

I place my hand on hers. "It's alright," I console, the corners of my lips lifting in a small smile. "It's not your fault. You were being kind and trying to help. I am truly grateful for what you did. I understand how terribly conflicted you were. You wanted to help me but at the same time you don't want to betray Brand. I know what he means to you."

"He's not evil," she cries passionately. "He's just led a very,

very hard life." Tears roll down her eyes. "He won't hurt you ... I know he cares about you. I see it in his eyes."

He has already hurt me, I want to say, but I do not. She wipes the tears off her face and holds on tight to my hand with both her hands. "Did you know that you and Brand share the same birth date?"

For a moment I am speechless, and then I shake my head in disbelief. "Are you sure?"

She nods.

The door is suddenly pushed open, and we both swivel our heads to see the devil in question. I feel my face flush guiltily. For the first time since I found myself a prisoner in his home I see Brand look awkward and unsure of himself. He glances from me to Lindy to the food tray and back to me. "I see you are eating. Good," he mutters, and exits the room.

My gaze connects once more with Lindy's. There is deep grief in her face. "You see, he is not a monster. He pretends to be one so that no one will dare pity him. He is hurting ... and without a clue of how to set himself free. In all the time I've known him I don't think I've ever seen him smile, a true smile." She touches her chest. "From the heart. If he does there's either sarcasm, or politeness, or worse, to indicate menace."

I'm startled when she suddenly grabs onto my hand with both of hers. "He's not a bad person. There are a lot of demons inside him, but he can be better. I don't know what the story is between the two of you, but one thing I know for sure. You are the most important thing he has in his life. I saw that when you were unconscious. He hung on to you so fiercely and protectively it was like watching a grizzly mother bear guarding its cub. He almost took a swipe at the doctor when he couldn't find your vein the first time, and had to try again."

"What do you want me to do?" My voice is full of torment.

"Help him," she pleads, "I beg of you. You are his only chance."

"How do I do that?"

"I have no clue," she admits sadly. "If I did I would give anything for it, but your heart knows. Your heart knows what to do. Listen to it."

She rises to her feet, and leans forward to brush the backs of her fingers down my cheek. "There's something wonderful and precious here. Don't walk away from it." Then she goes out of the door. I stare at the door for a long time, her words swirling in my mind.

Help him. Despite the confusion and the fear for my family I know that it is truly what I want to do. Maybe Lindy is right. Maybe I could help him. I do not for even one second doubt that it had been his full intention to frighten and make me submit by cutting off my father's finger, but something had made him hesitate, and only take his ring. I desperately want to believe I had something to do with his change of heart.

It will only be a matter of time before my father works out that my Spanish holiday is a complete lie. As soon as he does he will use every possible resource to find me. Before he finds me I must find a way to Brand's heart. I know there is going to be no happy ending for Brand and I. As much as it hurts to even think of ever parting from him. I know we must, but before we do I am going to do my very best to give him everything I have body and soul.

This will be my apology for hurting him all those years ago and triggering the chain of events that made his life into the miserable existence that Mrs. Parks came across.

CHAPTER TWENTY-EIGHT
Liliana

https://www.youtube.com/watch?v=nqnkBdExjws
-I will leave the light on-

*U*nable to sleep I wake up in the early hours of the morning and watch the sun rising, filling the horizon just beyond the moor with brightly colored hues of scarlet and a fiery tangerine. Even though it is perfectly magical with the carpet of snow on the ground it makes me feel sad. It's my birthday and I should be home with my family. I think of my mum. Thank God, she still thinks I'm having a tantrum in Spain and not being held hostage. I don't know if she could handle that.

I frown when I realize that I won't be able to keep this charade up much longer. Time is running out for me and Brand. The thought brings pain to my chest. Logically, I understand the state I am in is not favorable, but with each passing moment my reluctance to have it all come to an end keeps growing.

I've started to look forward to seeing him. Since he suddenly appeared and disappeared when Lindy was with me I've been waiting in earnest for him, my eyes constantly on the door, my heart jumping at the sound of every footstep in the corridor and sinking with each passing disappointment that it is not him.

I'm so engrossed in my thoughts my heart feels like it just about flies out of my chest at a sudden crashing sound of the door hitting the wall. I whirl my head around. He is standing there with a nerdy looking guy in a hoodie and slouchy jeans.

"Are you ready to make your call?"

"Now?" My parents will both be asleep.

His expression is closed and hostile. "If you're not ready we can always schedule it for another day."

"No, no, I'll make the call now," I say quickly and move away from the window towards the bed.

The young man opens a laptop that is connected to some kind of machine inside a briefcase. He types in a few commands, then looks up at me. "What's the number?"

I say my parents' home number aloud and he types it in.

"Liliana!" Dad calls out urgently.

Tears fill my eyes, as I hear how much terror is in his voice. "Dad," I try to say as confidently as I could, but my voice breaks and there is not a thing I can do about it.

"Liliana! Are you all right? Where are you?"

"I heard about the accident," I whisper, my mind going to the mangled image of his vehicle from the news report, and I have to fight back my tears.

"Are you all right?" he demands, his voice trembling with emotion.

"I'm fine," I respond.

"Then why the hell do you sound like that?"

"I just heard about your accident," I answer. "It shocked me."

"It was nothing. I'm fine. Where are you calling from?"

"I just wanted to call you on my birthday to tell you that everything is all right and I'm fine. Can I speak to Mum, please, Dad?"

"Hang on. She's right here."

"Mum," I say and tears begin to flow down my face.

"Oh, baby, I miss you so much," Mum sobs into the phone.

"Oh, Mum. You know I love you, right?"

"I love you too. When will you be coming home, honey?"

"I ... I ... I don't know yet. But soon. Please be patient okay. I just wanted you to know that I am fine and I will be back soon. Please tell Dad that there is no need to look for me. I will come back when I am ready."

Suddenly my mum starts sobbing her heart out. She is crying so hard she can't even speak. My father comes back on the phone. "Liliana, do you remember everything I taught you?"

"Yes, Dad."

"Can you tell me anything?" There is almost a note of pleading in his voice.

I close my eyes with sorrow. Oh, Dad. I would rather cut off my hand than tell you where I am. "I'll be home soon," I say quietly. "Please take care of yourself and Mum … I love you, Dad."

"Liliana!" he roars, but I look up at the kid in the hoodie and make a quick slashing motion with my hand to indicate that I want the call to be terminated. He complies immediately.

I stand and walk over to the window. I am certain now that my father has made it his sole mission to find me. Whether he believes my disappearance is by choice or not, my days of being MIA are numbered.

The young kid leaves with his equipment and I turn around to look at Brand. My eyes follow him as he shuts the door and heads towards me.

Brand is a regal man.

His gait is without haste as he strolls across the room, his hair thick and rich as velvet falls in soft waves. It is just long enough to brush his shoulders. Today he has not shaved and his stubble makes him look dark and dangerous. His sweater a thick rich beige and his slacks are jet black. In different places they take the shape of the virility and strength of his legs. His boots are heavy duty and black. I realize also that I no longer feel any fear at his presence. I am able to hold his gaze until I feel my heart begin to quicken.

"Happy Birthday, Brand," I wish softly.

He frowns.

"I never knew that we had the same birth dates."

There is absolutely no expression on his face except an insurmountable coolness. This is going to be so much harder than my silly fantasies.

"I got you a cake. Do you mind if we share a piece?" I say and start walking towards the cake that I got Lindy to bake and ice for me. I pop open the lid and turn around to look at him. He walks over to me and stands looking down at the cake.

Lindy has decorated the cake with little blue and pink flowers and the words: Happy Birthday Liliana & Brand.

"I've got some candles," I say hopefully.

He turns to look at me, his face grim, a vein pulsating in his throat. "What do you think we are? Boyfriend and girlfriend?"

I shake my head. "Of course not. It's just what people do on their birthdays. They light some candles, sing a birthday song, blow out the candles and make a wish. After that they cut the cake and eat a slice."

"I'm not people. I don't follow silly traditions."

"What do you follow?"

"I follow what my body tells me to do."

I stare deeply into his eyes with all the confidence I can muster. "And what does your body tell you to do?"

"My body tells me to wait for your recovery so that we can get back on track."

"On track with what? My death?"

"My end for you is not death, its misery." Just like Lindy said, his smile is borderline cruel.

I remain unfazed. I let a smile hover over my lips. "I once

read a book about a random land with dragons. They had a tradition: whenever someone saves another's life, he's responsible for him forever."

"Yes, that probably works well in a random land with dragons."

"I apologize, Brand, for everything my father and I did to you. From the depth of my heart, I apologize. From this moment on I choose to be your friend."

"Friend?" he drawls. "Spoken like a true Eden." He drags his finger across our names on the icing and turning to face me brings it to my mouth. I see it happen almost in slow motion. He smears the sweet cream on my bottom lip and waits for me to lick the cream before he bends his head and licks my tongue. Then he lifts his head and stares into my eyes. Hypnotized by his gaze I forget even to breathe.

"We will *never* be friends, Liliana Eden," he says quietly before he walks out of the door.

CHAPTER TWENTY-NINE
Liliana

I don't see Brand all day and that night Mark comes to my room and asks me to follow him. We go up a small wooden staircase to a flat roof where a helicopter is waiting.

"Where are you taking me?" I shout above the noise.

He grunts, pulls open the door, and looks at me with a menacing expression. The flight to London is accomplished without the exchange of a single word. When he pulls the door open again and grunts for me to disembark, I just climb out without protest. It is particularly icy and windy, and the chill seeps into my bones as we walk to a waiting black car. The car speeds off into the night. Half an hour later we quickly make our way up the white steps into a private plane.

Brand's wealth is surprising. He is just in his 24th year and no matter how capable he is, going from homeless to filthy rich in nine years does not sit well with me. For some reason I had expected him to be in the plane, but there is only an impeccably dressed, smiling hostess, who shows me to one of the seats. Seconds later she is back around with a plate of fruits.

"Where is Brand?"

"I'm sorry I have no idea."

"But is he not flying with us tonight?"

"No, Miss Eden. You are the only passenger."

I exhale. "Where are we going to?"

"Paris," she answers with a broad smile.

"What about passports and stuff?"

Her smile falters slightly, before it rights again. "Don't worry. Everything has been taken care of."

A meal is served once we hit cruising altitude. It is good food, but I can only pick at it without much interest. I do not know when I fall asleep, but a sudden turbulence jerks me awake about an hour later. Soon the pilot announces that we will be descending.

A man wearing a peaked cap is standing beside a blue Range Rover with blacked out windows on the tarmac. The back door of the car is open. He touches his cap as one of the men who had accompanied me in the plane escorts me down the steps. Once I am enclosed inside, he closes the door, and gets into the front seat. Neither man speaks.

I keep my eyes peeled on the illuminated streets of the city. I have travelled extensively with my father, especially around Europe, but I've always had a love for Paris. I consider it to be the most romantic city in the world. Soon we leave the city and go past an endless silhouette of street lamps.

It is well past midnight when we finally arrive at our destination. The door is pulled open for me to exit. I expected a villa of some sort, but to my surprise the car rolls to a stop outside a simple farmhouse built of yellow stones. The front is partly covered in vines.

"You will find everything you need in the house," the driver says to me just as we arrive at the front door. Then both men wordlessly exit the house and shut the door squarely behind me. I wonder if they will lock me in, but after I hear the car drive off I open the front door and go stand outside. The air is cold and eerily silent. I quickly go back into the warmth and lock the door.

For a brief second I feel the discontent of a real prisoner, but I quickly cheer myself up with the thought that the house itself is bright enough and actually quite cozy. I decide to take a quick tour. There is a big green couch in the living room and the walls are decorated with small framed murals of food. There is a large open fireplace. The numerous plants, and antique wooden cupboards placed at different positions all show that either too much thought was put into the décor, or not enough, but regardless, the space has an incontestable charm.

The kitchen is another storehouse of trinkets. The emerald green tiles and red wooden cupboards make it look like something out of an old painting. Copper pots and pans hang from the ceiling, and on the shelves are rows upon rows of small jars of at least a hundred different condiments and spices.

I find myself suddenly hungry so I head over to the fridge to see what I can forage. It is bursting with smelly cheeses, cured meats, sausages, jars of fat, and so much foreign food, I become truly overwhelmed. I immediately shut the door, and as I do, notice a basket of baked goods sitting on the counter. Taking the whole basket with me and snatching a bottle of red wine sitting next to it by the neck, I go and plop on the couch.

The house is eerily quiet, but I'm a bit hesitant to switch on the small TV in case it keeps me from hearing what is going on outside. To my delight I manage to find an English book amongst a collection of novels on a shelf, and begin to read while digging into the basket of baked goodies. Whoever baked them did an amazing job. The butter cake was to die for, and that was before I started on the pastries.

CHAPTER THIRTY

Brand

I walk in with Mark a few minutes after midnight, our coats dotted with falling snow.

"The second twin was awfully quiet," he comments, referring to the men we met earlier to do some business with, "do you think they'll be able to pull it off?"

"They better," I respond, my eyes already searching around the house. "They fucking better."

Perhaps she's upstairs, I think when there is no sight of Liliana.

"Anyway, Antoine called earlier but you couldn't take the call. He said they have a man who takes care of the house each day. He will be here tomorrow so you're free to give him your instructions. The fridge is fully stocked and there's a complimentary pastry basket from his wife waiting for you in the kitchen."

I turn to Mark, my eyebrows raised. "That's a lot of talking for you at a go."

He grins. "I'll be on standby in the cottage next door. Unless you have something else you want me to do?"

"No, it's all right. Get some rest."

With a quick nod he exits the house, and I am left alone.

Walking as softly as I can so that I can mute my approach, I head into the living room. And lo and behold! Liliana is sprawled carelessly across the sofa and fast asleep. Her hair is sweeping onto the floor and there are crumbs of cake around her face and on the floor. There is a book on the floor. It looks as if it has fallen out of her hands. I move around to the front of the couch, pick it up to place on the coffee table. Ah, the obligatory bottle of red wine.

Then I take a deep breath and ... let my eyes take in the splendid sight of her.

She is creeping into my heart. Slowly but soon it will be impossible to let go. Whether it is infatuation or love, it doesn't matter. All I know is that she is constantly on my mind. I hate to admit it, but the excitement of her presence in my life adds a livened gait to my step. It's now harder to get my blood boiling at the least thing.

I look down at her deep in slumber. She looks so sweet, so innocent.

I know her father must have started actively searching for her ever since I sent him the message, so this little getaway at an acquaintance's cottage is the best location while I plan what to do next.

I reach out my hand to touch her silky hair, but then stop myself. Until I sort out my feelings towards her, minimal contact is necessary. Turning around, I start to walk away.

Then I stop. I can't leave her sleeping there. She would get up with a stiff neck.

I find myself carefully lifting her into my arms. She makes a little purring noise and burrows closer against my chest. Then with superhuman strength, I place a cushion under her neck, cover her with a blanket, and walk away.

CHAPTER THIRTY-ONE

Liliana

I feel wonderfully warm when I wake up the next morning.

The taste in my mouth however is quite unpleasant thanks to all the cakes, pastries, and wine I stuffed myself with. It put me in such a stupor that I actually drooled during the night. Wiping the corners of my mouth, I look through a window and see it is full on snowing outside. It is only then I notice the thick blanket spread over me.

My heart skips a beat when I realize Brand must have arrived last night. Instantly, my feet land on the floor. Throwing off the blanket I rush up the stairs, only slowing down to inspect each room as discreetly as I can. I don't exactly want to show my eagerness to see him again. When every closed door has been searched with no signs of him, only a black suitcase and another smaller one with my name on it, I feel surprisingly deflated.

As I brush my teeth I look into my eyes and I can see the disappointment there. I freeze when I hear the front door opening. Hurrying back to the banisters, I peek down. A guy in snow boots and a furry hat is standing at the threshold. His hands are filled with grocery bags. He doesn't see me and heads straight to the kitchen. I run my fingers down my messy hair and follow him. My bare feet make no sound and I stand at the doorway and watch him unpacking the fruits and ready-made meals from his bags. He seeks out a fork, opens a container of what looks like potato salad, and helps himself to a piece.

Tossing the fork into the sink, and chewing noisily, he takes off his coat and throws it onto a chair, only to turn around and almost jump out of his skin in terror at the sight of me watching him.

"*Oh putain!*" he curses.

"I'm sorry," I immediately apologize, somewhat amused at how startled he is. He looks no older than me, and just a few inches above my height too. His cheeks are full and his effort to grow a beard most probably to cover his acne is not paying off at all. There's bits of disconnected facial hair everywhere and it all makes him seem so animated. I instantly know I will like him.

I dig up my rusty French and quickly introduce myself with a smile. "*Bonjour, Je m'appelle* Liliana."

"*Bonjour,*" he greets, his hand still on his startled heart. "*Je suis Pierre.*"

We stare at each other ... all awkward smiles and stances until he cracks up in laughter. It brings one out of me too, but when he attacks me with a splattering of French my amusement immediately disappears. "Oh, I'm sorry I don't speak French all that well." I crinkle my forehead. "Didn't pay attention during French classes. I think the only word I still remember is *merci*."

"And *bonjour and Je m'appelle*," he adds with a twinkle to his eye.

I grin. "And ... où sont les toilettes."

"Yes, very useful phrase," he agrees gravely.

"Oh, excellent. You speak great English."

"Not really, but I do know a little more than thank you, hello and where are the toilets?"

"It will be enough for me," I say with a smile and head over to the counter to inspect the food he has brought into the house. As he makes us thick strong coffee, I soon learn that he is the house and grounds keeper for the owners of the house. "They only say that a close friend come here for a short time so I am to help him out."

"Mmm," I exclaim, with the fork still in my mouth at the delicious salad. "This is really good. Did you make it?"

"No. I can only cook eggs. Antoine's wife made it."

"Hmm ... Did your employers tell you how long the guest will be staying?"

He shakes his head in response and downs his coffee.

"Monsieur Abe told a man would be living here. That is why I am so surprised to see you."

"You are his daughter perhaps?"

"Ah ... No ... We're just ...well, friends."

He looks at me with a knowing look. "Ah ... *friends*."

"We've known each other a long time."

"Of course." He rises then and heads over to the sink to wash the dishes.

"Will you be here all day?" I ask.

"No," he replies, "I'm here just to put the food, and wash a little, and then I go."

"Okay," I say foreseeing yet another gloomy day alone. With a sigh I take a long sip of my glass of kiwi juice and look on, my thoughts filled with Brand. I wonder if Brand will decide to come back while I am still awake. I keep thinking of the end of us. It isn't long now, I can sense it, but how are we to part ways? With one of us dead, on civil terms, or ... I don't have the confidence to consider it but I note the brief flutter of my heart before I am called again by Pierre.

"What events do you have lined up today?" Pierre asks.

I shake my head pitifully, and say in my best French accent, "Zero."

"It is too cold to go out anyway," he says.

I gaze out at the outer pool and hedges covered completely in snow. It looks beautiful, but I wish Brand would come back. "Pierre," I call.

He turns to me while rubbing his nose with the back of his hand. He deposits some soap suds on it and it extends his nose. He looks so funny I can't help laughing.

I rise and take my empty glass over to him. As he takes the glass from me, I ask, "Pierre, what do you do if you want to get close to someone?"

He pauses for a moment to think before he responds. "Spend time with them."

Fat chance of that happening when Brand has decided to become more evasive than a ghost. My face drops.

His smile almost blinds me. "You are in love?"

I nearly choke. I settle for a staggeringly hideous frown. "No, I am not."

My answer seems to genuinely confuse him. "Why do you want to be closer then?"

"I owe him ... a debt," I say.

"Then pay him," he says simply as if it is the most obvious answer in the world.

"You're no help," I say and return to my seat.

He wipes his hand and comes over to take the seat by my side.

"Okay, okay ... maybe it is more ... complicated," he says. "Spend more time with him."

"He doesn't want to," I explain. "Spend time with me."

He gives me a dry look and I almost don't want to hear it. He leans into me and says it anyway. "So, make him fall in love with you." He links his fingers together. "You are beautiful woman. It is easy."

"How exactly do you make someone fall in love with you?" I ask.

He leans back into the chair and raises up two fingers. "Two ways. Be helpless, or be mysterious."

Propping my elbow on the table, I rest my head against it, before it explodes with his strange advice.

"Helpless? What do you mean?"

"Do something that make him be forced to spend time with you. Like break your leg, or your arm."

Or go blind I add in my head. That would really up the ante.

He goes on. "Add to dis ... show him you are good ... exciting. Then maybe he begins to fall in love with you."

"So breaking my leg doesn't guarantee he will fall in love with me?"

To my surprise he takes the question seriously. "No. Fall in love is two other different things."

I curse myself for even asking in the first place.

If he expects me to break anything else I will break his leg, I say in my head.

"Poison him or make him jealous."

I blink, not sure that I have heard him well. "Pardon?"

"Joke," he says, laughing heartily, obviously beside himself at his humor.

I have none left in me.

"Make him jealous,' he says. "And he will begin to notice you."

I think about this for a moment.

"Or give him woman poison."

"Huh?"

"It's not joke."

"Woman poison?" I repeat, wishing I had never begun this conversation in the first place.

He shimmies his shoulders suggestively and lets his eyes drop to my breasts. I rise to my feet then, exhausted to my soul.

"Have a beautiful day," I say to him and leave the kitchen.

CHAPTER THIRTY-TWO
Liliana

I settle in front of the television with a bucket of popcorn to await Brand that evening. Dressed in a pair of jean shorts from my suitcase and an oversized dress shirt I found inside Brand's suitcase, I feel quite cozy and relaxed.

The evening passes away and I nod off to sleep. The next thing I know I've jerked awake. The lights are still on, and I look around, slightly disoriented to check the time. It is past 2.a.m in the morning.

I hear a sound upstairs and quickly hurry up the stairs. I rap my knuckles on the wood, and even though I don't receive a response, I take the liberty of pushing the door open and walking in. His room has a king-sized bed.

It looks mighty comfortable and reminds me of our first time together on a bed. A mini panic laced with hot-blooded desire instantly tries to bully me into turning away, but I stand my ground and keep walking forward.

"Brand?" I call tentatively.

As I near the bathroom I hear the sound of the shower running. Taking a deep breath, I push the door open. The clothes he wore that day are discarded on the tiled floor.

Through the frosted shower glass, I see the outline of his naked frame and my heartbeat starts to spiral out of control. What am I doing? This is Brand the Maniac I am intending on provoking. Have I gone mad? What has made me so fearless against someone who has threatened the lives of both my father and I? Then I think of Lindy saying he was like a mother bear with her cub when I was ill. He cares, but he hates himself for it. Before I leave I have to make him understand that I didn't reject him deliberately. That I always regretted doing it and wished with all my heart I could turn back the clock and change the way I acted. The sooner I make this better the sooner I can return to my family.

You're making this right, I remind myself. *You're trying to atone for past sins. You are doing this for you and him.*

Even telling myself that doesn't give me the courage to slide open the door and I find myself chickening out and turning around to exit the bathroom. I only manage two steps before I hear the shower stall door slide open. I freeze instantly on the spot.

His voice is as cold as steel. "What are you doing here?"

I am almost too afraid to turn around, but summoning all my courage I lift my chin and turn around to meet him.

CHAPTER THIRTY-THREE

Liliana

https://www.youtube.com/watch?v=crAgnI9BF6M
Simply The Best.

*H*e is standing in the doorway buck naked but for some water droplets. My eyes nearly pop out of their sockets as I let them really study the tattoos on his arms, shoulders, chest and stomach. For the first time I have the opportunity of seeing them clearly.

They are beautiful.

High on his right shoulder there is a black rose with teardrops falling from it. A fierce tiger roars on his chest. An angel is on her knees in front of a demon on his bicep. Around them there are knives and other symbols that must mean something to him.

Of its own will my gaze slides down his narrow hips to his

groin, to the virile,
tightly together to co

"I asked you a questic

My gaze flies up to h
"Um ... I ... uh ..." I st

He narrows in on wl
lidded. Alarm bells
instinctively taking a
unknown quantity.

I get my mouth to work
said you want me to be
what makes me even

I push my way
expression.
can stop
damp
th

"Did your little pussy get wet for me?" he asks nastily.

My jaw drops and he looks at me with a disgusted expression and slides shut the door of the shower so hard it makes me jump.

For a stunned second I can only stare blankly at the closed glass. He just outright rejected me! I offered myself to him and he rejected me. Confused and shaken, I turn around to leave, but then something inexplicable overtakes me. How dare he? How dare the bastard treat me like that when I am only trying to heal his hurt.

Well, woman's poison it will have to be. As Mum once said about Dad. No point trying to tame a wild beast better to embrace its magnificence.

I march over to the stall and forcefully slide the door open. His head bent and under the cascade, water is rolling down his silky skin. His back is wide and ripped with muscles that run all the way down to his firm ass. Billowing steam mists around him, making him appear almost unreal. My throat pulsates with thirst. He turns around, brushing hair out of his face.

before I can lose my courage. "You
miserable, well I am. But do you know
more miserable? You fucking me does."

into the stall and he looks at me with a strange
mixture of desire and exasperation. Before he
me, I begin to undo the buttons of my shirt, but it
well takes too long, so I rip it apart viciously. When
that doesn't take me far either, I pull the shirt over my head
revealing one of the sexy bras he bought for me. I take that
off too so the poison can take effect more quickly. My gaze
drops to his rising cock.

"That was a four-hundred pound shirt you just ruined," he
says quietly, but his eyes are focused on my bare breasts.

"I would have thought four hundred pounds would be
nothing to-" I start to say, but the words are stolen out of my
mouth when he takes a step forward. He is suddenly dangerously close to me. My heart is racing in my chest and I am
breathing too hard.

"Get out," he says, "before you regret it."

For the longest time there is no other sound, but the sound
of water pattering down to the floor and our quick uneven
breaths.

"I want to regret it," is all I say.

"You fucking little demon," he curses.

My heart flutters with fear and longing, but my hands go to
the button of my shorts. I pull them down along with the
thong he so thoughtfully provided. Kicking them aside, I
hold Brand's gaze as I close my hand around his cock.

"You're no longer afraid of me?" he asks softly.

"I'm terrified," I respond, "but I *need* you."

The curiosity vanishes and I see lust completely take over in his eyes. "Just remember you asked for this," he snarls.

As quick as lightning, I drop down to my knees and take the head of his cock in my mouth. I crawl on my knees with him as he staggers backwards against the wall. The warm water cascades down on both of us as I suck on the rock-solid length.

I still remember gagging the last time I tried this and how he had finished the job himself. With my hand at the root I swallow up his dick as deeply as I can, but before I can start to gag I pull away slowly, sensuously. I let my tongue run up and down the silky-smooth length, tracing the bulging veins before I lower my head to take his balls into my mouth.

He groans and I lay my palm on his flat belly. I can feel his pulse underneath his skin. Fast and slightly erratic. His cock grows bigger inside my mouth and it makes my heart swell with pride to know I can do this to him.

Almost beside myself with arousal and excitement I feel my stomach clench when his body starts to clench and contract. His hand slides around my neck to hold me in place, just where he wants. I pray I will not start choking like some amateur. Lifting my gaze, I see his head resting back against the wall. His eyes are shut with the intensity of emotions coursing through him.

With a smack he shuts the water faucet off.

I take him as deep into my throat as he will go. Drops of cum spill into my mouth and I lap it all up, craving his taste more than anything in the world. His hand spreads into my hair as he begins to rock his hips backwards and forwards. Holding me in place, Brand explodes inside my mouth, shooting straight down my throat. I suck wildly on the engorged head and hear his palm hit the tile wall just before his curse rings out in the enclosed space.

"*Fuck,*" he swears.

A groan escapes my lips. Everything about this man turns me on. He roughly pulls me up to him and at first I am unable even to stand. Brand gazes into my eyes and I cannot breathe.

"Did I do okay?" I whisper.

"What?" he rasps.

"Did I do okay?" I repeat

"Yeah, you did just fine," he says as he spins me around. He slams my back against the wall. His hands placed on either side of my face sting like burning coals. My hands slide around his waist to grab hold of him unwilling for even an inch of space to be between us. Slanting his head, he kisses me, *hard,* and my entire body goes limp.

His tongue takes over my mouth and I surrender to it all. By the time he pulls his lips from mine I cannot even open my eyes. All I can do is *feel*.

He goes to my breast and I feel my pussy drip even more. My own cream rolls warm and thick down my legs and I feel as if I am melting as his mouth tugs on my nipple. The painful pleasure rocks my whole body and my hand instantly goes between my legs. But Brand's hand arrives quicker, his fingers slipping in between the soaked folds as he palms me hard. I trap his hand between my legs and cry out at the beautiful torment.

"Fuck," I gasp, my toes curling.

He takes a nip of the skin between my neck and shoulder, and my knees buckle. Crazed with lust, I begin to trace kisses down his body, my aim is to brand all of him. He grips my waist in his hand and spins me around. My hands connect with the wet tiles, my face is pressed into the cool smooth wall. I shut my eyes as his hands roughly grab my hips and pull my hips back, making my buttocks jut out.

"Yes, yes, fuck me," I plead, writhing my ass against his groin.

His mouth rests against my ear. "Your mouth has turned dirty," he growls. Looking into my eyes, he parts my ass and sensually rubs his dick up and down my crack. My sex feels so swollen and hard I know I can climax any moment.

His hand slaps my buttocks hard and I cry out.

He kicks my legs to spread them further apart. I feel him lower his hard body slightly, then his cock head finds my opening. In one smooth movement, his whole cock plunges into me. I moan with the shocking pleasure. My fingers end up tangled in my own hair as he stretches and completely fills me out.

"Brand," I cry out, as he begins to move inside of me. Only the tips of my toes remain on the floor as I rise to meet his brutal thrusts. He seems angry as he pounds into me. I realize I don't want it any other way. This is how we connect. Like animals.

I can hear him panting behind me as he fucks me ruthlessly. His grunts are pure music to my ears and I relish each sound as his dick drives deeper and deeper into me. My scream is unconscious as I slam my buttocks into him. My hand goes to my clit to torture the already tormented nub in hard rapid circles. I lose all the strength in my body as wild pleasure begins to melt off all of my bones.

My feet leave the floor when I eventually explode. The whole world ceases to matter. There is only Brand's body rubbing against me, his voice grunting, his dick deep inside me. Brand holds me up against him as he comes together with me, the both of us gasping and trembling against the other. I feel his hot seed shooting into me.

Our bodies are slicked with sweat. The combined scent of our sex envelops us as we tremble with the force of our climax. He bites deeply into the skin of my shoulder and it just makes the juices flowing out of me increase.

It takes a while before either of us let the other go.

Brand leans against me, completely spent while my hands rest against the tiled wall. I want to kiss him before he comes to his senses so I angle my head and catch his lips with mine. He doesn't resist, his tongue dances and tangles with mine as we lap each other up. Eventually he spins me around to face him. I know it is over, but I don't want it to be.

I lick my lips slowly.

For a second his eyes are mesmerized by the journey of my tongue then his big powerful hands go around my buttocks. Grabbing my flesh he lifts me up. My legs automatically curl around his waist. I search his face until he captures my mouth again. His tongue is hot and velvety and the kiss is deep and passionate.

It is a shock to feel his cock slipping into me once more.

I did not think it was possible for a man to be able to go again so soon after, but I do not question the blessing. I shut my eyes and cradle my lover's head against my breasts.

Brand slams into me and we begin our dance all over again.

Lost in his embrace, I never want to find myself again. As my nails dig into the skin of his back, my entire body moves back and forth with the force of his fucking, I swear to myself that I will make him mine. I already seem to have ruined him for anyone else, anyway. I just have to remove the barrier that he has erected between us.

He may be a fucking maniac, but he is my maniac.

I clench down hard and mark his satiny skin as he takes me to the edge of the cliff once more. Brand searches for my lips and kisses me so hard we breathe through each other's mouths.

I feel tears fill my eyes as my entire body quickens with my impending orgasm. The heat from his body radiates in waves and consumes us both. He comes with me once again, his cry is animalistic, his hips slamming painfully into me. I throw my hands around his shoulders as our bodies tremble against each other.

His head falls in the crook of my neck as he fights to control his breathing. I savor this moment of silent communion between us. I wish it could last forever, but the dream is broken when he tugs on my legs clamped around his hips. I loosen them and my legs fall from around him and back to the ground.

I wait, almost afraid to breathe, as I brace myself for the rejection that I already know is coming. It comes in four heartbreaking words.

"You can go now," he says watching me intently.

I pretend to shrug, insouciant as a cat. "Sure, why not? I've got what I came for," I say airily as I pull the door open and let myself out. I try not to hurry away now, achingly aware of my nakedness and his eyes boring holes through me as I take my leave. Soon I am out of the room. Naked, I hurry to my room and collapse on my bed. I pull the covers over my head and try, just try to breathe.

"It will all be okay," I promise myself. "Just breathe."

In out. In out. In the end I start to shiver with the cold. A brutal shard of pain digs itself into my chest. No matter how horrible Brand is to me, I cannot rid him from my heart.

CHAPTER THIRTY-FOUR

Liliana

https://www.youtube.com/watch?v=aYr4fDuLhXg
Without Me

The next morning I am awoken by the sound of something falling close to my face. Startled, I open my eyes to see Brand staring down at me. He is fully dressed in a calf-length coat, buttoned up black silk shirt and trousers, his hair has been combed back, and his jet-black beard is trimmed. He looks as deliciously wicked as sin.

For the first few moments he doesn't speak and I let my eyes take in the thing next to my head.

"Take the pill," he says to me.

I sit up, push my hair out of my face, and regard him. "I will."

He nods then turns around to leave and I remember that I am meant to treat him with total kindness. Unconditionally, and selflessly. This is my apology.

"Thank you for thinking of me," I say.

I might as well have been talking to the walls since he exits the room without even a glance back. I fall back on the bed. I don't know how I can possibly help him. No matter what Lindy thinks he makes his wish of wanting absolutely nothing to do with me pretty blatant. I know it will be time for me to leave soon, but even imagining going back to my old life is impossible. It is almost as if I was a different person then and I cannot walk into her life. It would be too boring. Too empty. I think of my mother and feel sad for her. If only there was a way for me to have Brand and my family in my life. Of course, that would never happen, not when he hates my family so strongly.

Pierre arrives an hour later while I am eating my breakfast of yogurt and fruit in the kitchen. The truth is I'm barely even tasting any of it.

"*Bonjour*," he says to me and his bright eyes draws a smile out of me.

"Bonjour," I greet listlessly.

"All is well?" he asks, an eyebrow cocked.

"Yeah."

He doesn't seem to believe me and presses on. "Was the poison used on the wrong someone?"

I look up. "What?"

He nudges his chin over to my neck and gives me a sly smile. Shit. I immediately jump to my feet. While he laughs I hurry around the kitchen looking for a mirror till Pierre pulls one out of a drawer and hands it to me.

I snatch the intricate brass frame from him and peer into it.

A red hickey is evident for the world to see, and I feel myself turning a bright shade of pink. Pierre comes over with a slice of cheese and takes the seat at the table.

"So," he says, "if poison not work we go to the next strategy. Make him jealous."

The idea already sounds mighty ridiculous to me. Even the thought of Brand being jealous of me sounds like a fantasy. He'll probably find it very amusing to think that anyone could imagine he would be jealous of my activities.

"Find a good-looking man," Pierre is saying. "Seduce with him just a bit, and let your ... *friend* find the two of you in flagrante delicto."

"Isn't that a rather dangerous strategy? Couldn't it lead to violence?"

He shrugs. "I'll take the risk."

I grin. "Are you proposing to put yourself forward as the good-looking man?"

"Yes, I can help you. Tonight, I serve at a new bakery's open soirée. Come with me, look beautiful, and have a bit of fun. When you come home your friend will be hot for you."

I think about how easily I could run away from Brand, but incredibly there is not a single cell in my body that wants to leave him. I also realize that Pierre has no idea how dangerous what he is suggesting is. Brand is not a man to be played with. If he thinks Pierre is helping me to escape there could be hell to pay for him.

"You might get in trouble!" I say mildly to him.

"What trouble?"

"Forget it. Too dangerous."

He rises to his feet in disappointment. "You're ... how do you say it in English, cluck, cluck, ah yes! *chicken*." He sits back down and looks at me with a smug expression.

"I'm not afraid to go," I say quietly.

"Then come with me to the soirée. Push him just a little, see what happens?"

More than ever I am certain that Pierre is the devil because how in the hell can I say no to such a possibility? Anyway, judging from Brand's past behavior he won't come back until well past midnight, and as long as I'm back well before that I should be fine.

"I need to be back by ten o'clock though."

Pierre's grin is wide. "No problem."

"I mean it."

He lifts one shoulder and lets it drop. "By eight o'clock the whole area is dead anyway."

At 5.00 p.m. sharp, I am dressed warmly and ready to go. Pierre has just finished up cleaning the living room so he appears at the back door to put on his coat. "You ready?" he asks.

I nod.

"Those men who wait outside. Are they ... guards?"

I nod. "Yeah. We don't have to go, you know."

He grins, his eyes full of mischief. "So we will exit out of the cellar window. No one is there." He opens a rickety door by the larder and we go down into a dark cold cellar. The air smells of fruit and alcohol. Using the light from his phone, we climb out of the window.

"Wait here," he orders, a thrill of excitement in his voice.

I hear his rusty little Renault start and drive away. The air is freezing cold and just as I start to wonder if he has just played a little joke on me, he appears at the side of the house.

"Let us go," he says.

He leads me past the pool, and down a dark little path until we emerge onto the main road. Further down I see his red Renault parked in the bushes. We climb into his car and both of us start laughing. Our noses are running and our lips are so frozen we can barely laugh, but it is exciting to think we just evaded Brand's men. I squash away the prick of guilt at the kind of trouble they would be in if Brand found out by telling myself we will be back long before Brand gets back. We drive down to what appears to be a small town.

Soon we arrive at the bakery having its opening. A small crowd of people are gathered inside. We get in and I find that it also doubles up as a stunning cafe. A carousel of all of their delicacies running through the middle of the room. At the sight of pastries and whipped cream, Brand and all my troubles are immediately forgotten.

"Have fun," Pierre says to me and I do not need to be reminded. "I will be in the back working. Come find me if you need me." I nod excitedly to him and grab a Mascarpone and Raspberry Rose Cream Choux Pastry. It is generously filled with cream patisserie, but my eyes catch yet another crafted exactly in the form of a Rubik's cube.

I go after it shamelessly.

CHAPTER THIRTY-FIVE

Brand

*M*ark is speaking as we walk into the house, so it takes me a few minutes to notice that something is wrong. I stop suddenly and look around, my eyes narrowing. Mark stops speaking and glances around too.

"I'll go check," he says as he begins to lightly run up the stairs.

I head into the living room. As I suspected there is no one here.

"She's not up there either," Mark announces, before immediately backing away. "I'll ask the guards," he says, before he runs out of the house. I wait. Lowering my head, I shut my eyes at the sudden surge of anger that shoots through my body.

A few minutes later Mark returns through the door with an update. "They're searching the property. We'll find her, Boss," he tries to reassure me, but I am past listening.

"Get me everyone on duty," I order and he hurries off. A few minutes later, all six men file in. My call to Antoine, the house's owner connects in that moment.

"Is there an alternate way out of your home?" I ask him.

He is silent for a few moments. "Why?"

I understand his caution. We're both programmed to be wary of even the closest of acquaintances. "My girl is gone."

"There is," he immediately confirms. "Through the cellar, but only Pierre has the key."

The boy ...

Shit! That little wet-behind the ears kid, but it makes perfect sense. He has been Liliana's companion in the house. It would have been so easy for her to manipulate him. I think of her winding her arms around his thin wiry frame, offering her body to him, opening her white thighs, and my blood boils.

"I'll call you back," I say to him and end the call.

I quickly place another call to the boy, but there is no response.

Before I can stop myself my hand has flung the phone towards the wall, but it hits one of the men squarely in the head and shatters into pieces. Blood trickles down his face. I watch as he struggles to keep his balance, his hand over his head.

Apart from him, the rest remain at attention as I fight to control my breathing; I am heaving with such uncontrollable fury I want to kill someone.

"Find her," I growl, and even before I bend down to pick up my handgun, the room has emptied.

CHAPTER THIRTY-SIX

Liliana

Thirty minutes later I start to worry. I have stuffed myself with more sweets than I care to recall, but my mouth is bitter with fear. I shouldn't have come and certainly not with Pierre. What the hell was I thinking? Brand is not a man to be trifled with.

If I am going to disappear then it better be all the way back to England in search of my dad, who knows exactly how to protect himself, otherwise this potentially puts a lot of people in trouble. I go to find Pierre, and catch sight of him through the kitchen door washing dishes. The decision to go in is taken away from me when one of the uniformed bakers points me to the sign at the door that says only employees allowed.

I turn away then and try to relax to the classical music playing through the speakers. An hour later I cannot take it anymore. I plead with one of the waiters to bring Pierre out and the moment he comes running out of the kitchen, I address him.

"I need to leave now."

He looks towards the kitchen and then back to me. "I still have one hour on my work."

"It's alright," I say with a smile. "I'll take a cab home. Could you please give me the address?"

"Non, non, non," he refuses, "just wait one hour and I will be finished."

"Trust me, Pierre. I need to leave now. We might truly get in trouble if I stay any longer."

"That's the plan!" he cries confidently. "Make him jealous. I go with you so he sees me dropping you off. Believe me he will be extremely jealous."

"I'm really not sure about this, Pierre."

"Trust me. I am a man. I know how men think. We are all apes inside."

"I think I just want you to call a taxi," I say, anxiety growing in my voice.

He shakes his head. "Just wait here for me, okay? I will try to hurry as much as possible. I promise I will get you back by 9.30 latest."

I nod because I need to think. He smiles and rushes off towards the kitchen.

Pierre thought his plan would make Brand jealous, but I know that there is no chance in hell of that happening. Agitated because he thought I had escaped? More like down-right murderous? Yup, we are going to pull that off with a bang.

I pick up a glass of wine and drain the entire glass in one go. I then take a deep breath and buckle my nerves in to last until the end of Pierre's shift.

At fifteen past nine, Pierre pulls up his Renault and for a moment I do not want to come out. It is unusual not to see any guards outside, and it increases my wariness.

"Thanks for taking me, Pierre. You better get home now," I say, but he gives me an amused look and gets out of the car and comes around to my side.

"I thought you were going to drop me off and leave."

"I am, but first I am going to escort you to the front door."

I sigh. I guess it is better he is with me so that I can have some control over the situation. Away from me, and I cannot guarantee his safety.

A rude awakening awaits Pierre when we walk into a room that is colder than the wintry night beyond. It seems like an army is in the room and at the center of it all is their general, with a glare that is ready to draw blood.

His gaze moves between me and Pierre before finally settling darkly on Pierre. I can tell Pierre feels every bit of the tension in the room. All his cheeky confidence is gone and he instantly begins to explain himself, his English far worse than it has ever been. There is even a slight stutter thrown in the mix. Brand remains seated, impassively staring at Pierre's face.

"Mademoiselle Liliana ... uh ... f-felt very alone, so uh ... I have a job, another one from this ... uh ... patisserie and ... so I take her with me."

Brand rises to his feet and a split second later Pierre is staring down the barrel of a hand gun. I almost scream out in fright at the sudden appearance of the weapon, my hand clapping over my mouth. Pierre goes white as a sheet. He is trembling so much I can actually see his hands shaking.

I immediately jump in front of the gun my arms spread out in his defense. "Brand," I cry. "Don't blame him. I pleaded with him to take me out. There was a bakery opening tonight and since he works there. I just needed to breathe for a little whil-"

"If you don't move I'm going to send the bullet through the both of you," Brand says with cold narrowed eyes. I don't doubt he will do it, but I turn around and throw my arms around Pierre's as a shield. Nothing can happen to him on my behalf. I hear the cocking of the gun and tremble even more than Pierre does. Tears start running down his eyes.

"Get this fool out of here," I hear Brand say coldly, and we both nearly collapse at his words.

Two of his guards come over and roughly manhandle Pierre out of the room. I watch him leave and then turn around to glare at Brand. I am still shaking with shock. I march towards him, and in front of the rest of his guards, swing the hardest slap that I can towards his face.

His reflexes are lightning quick and he catches my wrist and twists my arm. "Did you just try to hit me?" he asks, almost in disbelief.

"What is wrong with you?" I scream. "What is fucking wrong with you? Why do you do this to people?"

"Get out," he tells his men. In seconds we are alone.

"So I went to a bakery and ate some French desserts," I taunt. "What are you going to do about it, huh? Are you going to kill me? Yeah? Then you better do it right now otherwise I'm going to be the one to kill you because you're fucking insane. Do you hear me Brand? You're fucking out of your mind. Are you even human anymore?"

With a strong tug I break his hold on my wrist.

"Fuck you," he says, turning around to head up the stairs.

I don't even think. I am like a crazed person. I go after him taking the stairs two at a time to catch up to him. I don't even know what I want to say to him, all I feel is this ball of frustration and anger that feels like it is going to kill me so the moment I get to him at the landing I just start hitting him like I am some sort of robot or machine that is malfunctioning. I pound his back and kick him with all my might. He turns around, grabs me and drags my body so close to his it is no longer possible to punch or kick out.

"Fuck, Liliana, are you trying to provoke me further?" he spits furiously.

"Provoke you further to what?" I ask. "You've been dreaming of killing me for years. Go on. Do it. I dare you," I say.

He grabs my neck with a hand and suddenly I am held in a chokehold. "Stay away from me," he warns as angry tears roll down my eyes and splatter on his hand. He pushes me away then, lightly, but it is more than enough to send me staggering backwards. I try to right myself, but my foot meets nothing, and before I know it I am tumbling down the stairs.

I try to latch onto something, but the only thing within my grasp is empty air. All I can see is Brand's eyes widened in horror. I watch it all almost in slow motion. Brand comes after me but it is too late.

I tumble down the rest of stairs. All I see is Brand's coat billowing out behind him as he tries to catch me.

Then my head hits the hard ground and I see actual stars.

CHAPTER THIRTY-SEVEN

Brand

*W*atching her tumble down the stairs, her eyes fixated solidly on me fills me with such acute fear my insides shake like jelly. I don't even feel this when my own life is in danger. Maybe because I accepted I won't live a long life. In my profession, it is damn well baked in the cake. Live by the sword die by the sword.

But the thought of Liliana dying is like the whole world turning black.

Thankfully, she passes out for just a few minutes. With my heart in my throat, I gather her into my arms and her eyelids flutter open. She blinks then tries to focus on me. I stare at my fiery angel, my mind in turmoil. I don't know why she pushes me to such uncontrollable rages, but I cannot bear it when I hurt her.

"I'm so sorry," I whisper hoarsely. The words tumble out on their own accord, even though I cannot remember the last time I apologized to anyone.

Her fingers grab my shirt and she refuses to let go, holding on with all her might, even though she is barely conscious.

With her secure and safe in my arms, I rise to my feet and go back up the stairs. I lay her on my bed and, releasing her fingers from my shirt, run my hands over her body. She appears not to have broken anything. The relief is palpable I cannot get rid of the sinking feeling in the pit of my stomach. We cannot continue like this. One of these days I'm going to end up hurting her.

I stand and pace the floor restlessly. Liliana will be my salvation and destruction.

She calls my name and I go and lie next to her. I can smell the cakes she has eaten on her breath and something inside me breaks. I am destroying her. I convinced myself that was what I wanted, but I know now it is not. It is not. No, I don't want to break her. I want to keep her. Dare I admit it, love her. I place my hand lightly on top of her and watch as she drifts in and out of sleep, my heart beating harder and faster than it ever has. I cannot stop looking at her, breathing her in, inching my way closer and closer towards her. She is mine. All mine.

Her hair is all over the place and I brush it gently away from her beautiful face. She talks a little in her sleep … indecipherable musings that make me hurt. I have given her so much grief … so much pain. It's time I stop. I don't care about taking revenge anymore. It was a destructive goal that I held on to for too long.

Of course, it was not her fault that my mother died.

I was a kid. I couldn't deal with the guilt. I needed someone to blame. To hate. But the truth is I never really hated her. I had to talk myself into it. The closer I got to her, the more hateful I had to force myself to be. I can remember that day I stole a kiss from her like it was yesterday. I knew even then she was mine. I was willing to pay any price to have her then. No one could have convinced me to drop her. Not my father, not my mother.

It was fate that intervened.

She is fine this time. There will be no more next time. I won't let her push my buttons so easily again. Never again. Anyway, I will have a doctor over in the morning to properly check on her.

There is one thing that I want to know more than anything else. Why she did not leave. She was with the boy, she could have found her way back and far away from me, possibly even out of my reach forever, but she came back. She doesn't know it, but she just stopped a war between Crystal Jake and me. We would have fought to the death.

My mind goes back to her promise on my birthday. At the time, it was all nonsense being sputtered, but now I shut my eyes and take a deep breath. It is too risky to hope ... No, I won't do that to myself.

I open my eyes a few seconds later ... and get a shock.

Her bright blue eyes are open and she is staring intently at me. There are a thousand things that go through my mind in that moment, but more than anything, I realize I am bare. Everything I am feeling; the longing, the confusion, the fear, the terrible guilt, it's all in my eyes and she can see it all. I have never been so exposed. It feels strange. I begin to move away, but she grabs my shirt with both her hands.

I gaze at her pale knuckles.

She moves until her face is right up to mine and her eyes are boring deeply into mine. I feel as though I am about to break. "Stay with me, Brand," she whispers. "Don't leave. Please."

This woman is a witch. The world I carefully constructed around me is falling apart. I know I should go. I am already in too deep. I *have* to go, I *need* to go, but somehow I cannot get myself to move. I fall onto my back in defeat, and she sprawls across me.

She rests her head on my chest and winces.

"What hurts?" I ask lifting myself on my shoulder and looking at her worriedly.

She smiles. "My head, but I kinda deserve it."

I slip my fingers through her silky hair. I know exactly where the bump is and she lets out a little yelp of pain when my fingers touch the swelling. "You'll see a doctor tomorrow. Let me go get you some painkill-"

She grabs me suddenly and refuses to let go. "I don't need a couple of Aspirins, Brand. I need you."

Once again, I am pulled down into her delicious magic, her warmth and scent slowly intoxicating me, rendering me completely void of any kind of will. She has complete control over me and I realize with shock nothing has ever scared me so much.

"Why did you come back?"

"I never left. There is nothing here but French TV. I was bored. I wanted your attention."

"You have quite a way of getting my attention," I say drily.

Her hands caress my chest, and it is anything, but relaxing. I catch her wrist, forcing her to stop. I can't take anymore. I am so close to pleading with her to have me ... in any way that she wants. This is not the way things are meant to go. Never have I felt so defeated by my own body. I was always someone with iron control. There is nothing that I can't say no to. Until her ...

She comes even closer to me and begins to nibble lightly on my chin. My breath escapes in a rush. God, I want her so fucking much it hurts. She begins to trace cake-scented, butterfly kisses down my neck and on to my chest. Her hands are busy loosening the buttons of my shirt.

Liliana lifts herself over me and in the next instant she is sitting astride me.

I close my eyes to try and stop the tide of emotions. "You shouldn't be doing this," I say, but I am not certain if I am speaking to her or myself.

"Why shouldn't I?"

I open my eyes and her face is barely an inch away from mine. She covers my lips with hers. Her lips are so soft and sweet. My mouth opens and she slips her warm tongue in. Liliana Eden kisses me with such passion that I feel myself go limp. My hands are on her waist underneath her blouse, and moving back and forth on the warm soft flesh. I can be in this state forever, with her on top of me, her hips slowly grinding on my rapidly swelling cock.

I want to speak to her about keeping her forever, but I know that there is too much against us. The high and mighty Jake Eden will never let an uneducated, common criminal have his daughter. Although since I know his history the irony is not lost on me. I did not imagine choosing someone to solely belong to me, especially after what my mother's death did to my father, but right now and in this moment, all I want is Liliana Eden. Forever.

She pulls my shirt open and begins to trace those wonderful little kisses down my chest. I revel in the intriguing magic that is purely her.

"Take my top off," she instructs against my skin.

"Don't you feel pain?" I ask, as I catch the ends of her blouse.

"Ow," she says, her eyes widening slightly with pain.

I freeze. "Are you okay?"

"Stop being such an old woman and get my top off," she orders with a chuckle.

The things she says to me. Unbelievable. Any other woman would have already been out of the door. I pull the material over her head and fling it away. She leans into me for another kiss and I lose my train of thought and literally sink into her kiss.

"Take my bra off," my gypsy princess whispers into my mouth.

I do exactly as I am told and pull the black scrap of lace gently away. Her breasts pop out. I stare at them hungrily. I am being completely controlled, but I have never been so willing. I open my mouth to take her nipple between my teeth. Nipping at the swollen bud, I suck deeply on it as I fill my hand with the other mound. Squeezing and worshipping my third favorite part of her body. I do not even know when that information slips from my mouth.

She giggles. "Third? That's it?"

I truly did speak aloud. Damn I am losing control, but honestly, it is as if I am under a spell. My head is underneath her chin and I feel like a child being cradled in the sweetest of bodies. I lift her away from me slightly and look into her eyes. She takes a nip at my nose. "What then is your favorite part of my body?"

"Your mouth," I say, taking her bottom lip into my mouth and sucking on the soft luscious flesh. The pull on my groin is excruciating and I move her hips to soothe the ache. I slip my tongue into her mouth to dance against hers. It's a wild gypsy kiss. I drink in every ounce of her. The taste of her beats anything else in this world.

"My mouth," she says softly, as she pulls away from me her eyes sparkling.

It's as though I am looking down at myself when I look down at her. She is me. Where her skin ends and mine begins is impossible to tell. I am so unbelievably smitten. I pull her close to me again, unable to stand even that tiny separation even though the girl is sitting right on top of me. I trace my nose up her chest and to her neck luxuriating in her scent. She is wearing no fragrance, but her natural smell is better than any scent created by man.

"And the second favorite part?" Her voice is teasing and play-ful. I love her like this. If only we could always be like this.

I kiss her again. It is almost as if I have starved myself of her for so long I cannot be without her taste. She complies for a while before pulling away.

"Tell me," she pouts.

I feel my heart swell to bursting. "How are you so fucking beautiful?" I find myself muttering, and for a moment she stops. Stroking my hair, she whispers into my ears. "You're not too bad yourself, you know."

Tightening my arm around her waist, I hold her to me as I roll her in one smooth movement and deposit her on the bed. I unbutton her jeans and quickly tug them down her hips. Grabbing the ends of the material I yank them off her legs. She gasps when my mouth covers her sweet pussy.

"This," I growl. "This is my second favorite part."

She has on a matching lace underwear through which I suck on her swollen clit. She is so wet and ready. I lap up her juices while she writhes and twists like a cut snake, and then I push the material aside and slip my tongue into her opening.

"Take it off," she pants as she cradles my head in her hands.

"No, I want to see your little wet pussy with the string of your thong caught in between the folds of flesh.

"You're just a pervert, aren't you?" she says with a pout.

"A pervert. That's me." With my eyes on her I palm her and her mouth falls open at the sweet pressure. I slip my fingers into her and soon I am plunging in and out of my woman. Her eyes fall firmly shut as her hips grind vigorously to the motion of my fingers. Then I return my mouth to her cunt to eat her out.

"*Brand*", she cries.

The sound is pure music to my ears. Then as I make it my sole mission to drive her out of her mind with my tongue, her eyes roll into the back of her head and she begins to curse. Hell, the woman has a vocabulary that would make a sailor blush. Her arms hit the bed and her hands pull at the sheets to contain herself until she finally explodes. As her climax tears through her, I let her thighs trap my head.

There's no other place I'd rather be so I drink in her scent and enjoy the tremors of her orgasm, and when she is done I suck her very, very gently on her sensitive clit to soak up all the release from her climax. When I pull away there are tears in her eyes.

"See," I murmur, "why it's such a favorite of mine."

She kisses me hard, and moves instantly to loosen my trousers, unable to wait any longer.

I would have assisted her, but she seems immensely impatient, and brushes my hand aside. Soon I am unzipped, and my dick is stroking her wet pussy.

"Do you want to use a condom?" I ask.

She shakes her head. "No." Her star-burst eyes fierce and determined. "Never again."

She reaches for me confidently and acts as though she owns every part of me, no holding back whatsoever, no reservations. I have absolutely no complaints, especially when she turns her back on me and slowly impales herself on me. It turns me on even more to see her slight body swallow my cock. She spreads her legs further apart and bounces her ass slightly to drive me even deeper in.

When her head falls backwards and her hair cascades down her back I become convinced she truly is a siren sent to lure me. With her hands on my thighs for support, she begins to ride me, savoring every movement. Once she glances back and I am stunned by the expression on her face. It is that of a powerful Goddess, full of secrets. I watch, fully entranced as she chases her pleasure.

It's hard to believe that just a few days ago, she had never even been touched by a man. I was her first, and I am going to be her last. No one else will ever lay their hands on my woman. I cannot even fathom it.

She fucks me with an expertise that shows her to be a natural lover, her rhythm hard and fast, then excruciatingly slow. It is hard for me to hold back, but I want her to come again. The racing of my heart begins to spiral out of control, but I can see that she is panting heavily too. I won't have to plan it. This dance between us, is agonizingly, beautifully choreographed by the heavens.

She calls out my name again and again, her hips riding me wildly. I bury my own roar in her back when she pushes me over the edge and burst inside her, filling her with my seed. My mouth clamps down on her sweet flesh, even though I try my best to be careful not to mark her too brutally. When I collapse back on the bed though, I can clearly see the mark that I have left on her.

She allows herself to fall on top of me. Our bodies slick with sweat slip and slide. I immediately turn her around to face me. I want to cradle her. She lays my head on her chest and I feel my heart almost burst with a feeling of possession.

"Do you still hate me?" she whispers.

"No, Liliana, I don't hate you. I never really did. I just told myself I did because I couldn't stand the pain of knowing you didn't want me."

She lifts her head, her eyes pierce me. "Oh, but I always wanted you, Brand Vaughan. I was just shocked by the kiss. The way it made me feel. If you had only been less intense things would have been completely different."

"When we wake up you can tell me what happened to you after you left our house, okay?"

"Okay."

Just before I fall deeply I wrap my arms tightly around her. No matter what happens I will never let her go.

CHAPTER THIRTY-EIGHT

Brand

9 years ago

https://www.youtube.com/watch?v=FywSzjRq0e4

They took me to a hostel. A place where children are kept until a foster home can be found for them. I think I was too shocked to notice anything. I didn't see the gleam in the hostel owner's eyes when the policeman said, "Got another one for you. This one has no papers. Gypsy boy."

Mr. Havant showed me to my room. It was in the basement.

I didn't notice the blacked-out window or the bars over it either. And when he locked the door from the outside I hadn't thought to protest. I sat on the mattress in the dark in a disbelieving daze.

All I could think of was my mother. It seemed impossible she was really dead. It had all happened so fast. But what if she wasn't really dead? What if we had made a mistake? There were many stories told from ancient days of people who woke up from the dead. That was why we Irish, hold a wake. We stay up all night and hope it was all a terrible mistake and the dead would come back to life.

Who will hold a wake for my mother?

And my father? He handed himself to the men who he had spent his whole life detesting. They were the pigs. We never trusted them.

It was only when I decided to escape and go look for my mother that I suddenly noticed the metal bars on the windows and the door was locked from the outside. Now, I had a different problem to worry about. Something was not right. I was supposed to be in a home with many other boys. Instead I had been locked up alone in a dank basement.

Warily, I looked around. There was only a single bed with a thin mattress and no sheets. I realized I had become a prisoner. I sat back down on the bed. It stank of stale urine. The Havant man had said he would bring me a meal later. He was a puny man. I was only fifteen, but I knew I could overpower him easily.

I decided to wait for my meal to arrive and play it by ear then, but no meal arrived. The light switch did not work and I was soon sitting in a total darkness. Eventually, I heard footsteps on the stairs. I stood up, ready to ambush the man and escape from my prison. The door opened and before I knew it I saw a blue light flash into the room before I felt my whole body start convulsing with electricity. I screamed with pain as I fell to the ground my body jerking uncontrollably.

He had just tazered me.

I was still in agony on the floor when other men came into the room. The tazer had taken all of my life force and I could not resist the men when they opened my mouth and dropped a bitter white powder in it. I didn't know what it was and I tried to spit it out, but they held my nose and mouth shut and forced me to swallow the powder. Then they left.

As soon as they went I wiped my mouth clean with the ends of my shirt. At first I didn't feel anything, but as time went on something strange started to happen to me. I started to feel as if I was drunk. As more time passed, I realized I couldn't move my limbs. I had absolutely no control of my body at all.

A heavy-set woman with gray hair came into the room. She was carrying a bucket of something that had steam coming off it. Under her armpit was a couple of towels. She undressed me and washed me with soapy water. The whole time she never spoke or looked me in the eye, but treated me as if I was a doll or an inanimate object. As she washed my private parts I hated it, but there was not a thing I could do about it. After that she dried me and dressed me in a black rubber costume. It was like a one piece, but something a man would never wear. It was so tight she was sweating by the time she had dressed me.

She combed my hair, then put lipstick on my lips. I wanted to scream at her, but I was completely frozen. Not even the slightest bit of sound could I make. Men came in and carried me out. We travelled in a van. They were coarse men. They spoke lewdly about my body. They even touched my penis. I was carried into a grand house. It was clear someone of great importance lived in that house. I was put into a lift and taken into the basement of the house. The room I was taken to had red walls and a bed that was covered in pure white fur. The funny thing about the drug I had been given was that I could not do a thing with my limbs, not even my eyelids could I close, but every sensation was heightened. I could almost feel every silly individual stand of fur.

The men left. After a while a man with silver hair came in. His skin was so white it was like the underbelly of a lizard or a frog. He had a cocktail in his hand. He looked at me with a crooked smile on his face.

"My, my, what a great big cock you have," he said, taking a sip of his drink.

He left his civilized ways the moment he put his empty cocktail glass down. Then he became an insatiable animal. Ripping my costume apart. He treated me as if I was a sex robot. The abuse was unbelievable. He bit my cock so hard tears started to flow from my eyes. Watching me cry helplessly made him laugh with delight. He stuffed his pale penis into my mouth and fucked me so long I thought I would die.

It was a night from hell.

Then his friends arrived. A rough bunch in suits. They took turns. I felt it all. Like being stabbed again and again in the ass with a knife. The whole time I couldn't do a thing. Every time one of them mounted me I thought of Liliana. Her flowing dark hair, her beautiful blue eyes, her creamy skin, her musical voice, the delicious taste of her mouth. And I hated her more and more.

When I started to bleed, they laughed and said, blood was the best lubricant. I told myself. One day, I will make you bleed too, Liliana Eden. You'll see.

One day ...

CHAPTER THIRTY-NINE

Brand

*E*ven before I open my eyes I already know I am alone.

There is no warmth around me and when I open my eyes to the daylight filtering through the window, I know that Liliana is no longer around. I sit up, refusing to panic, refusing to feel any fear. She cannot leave the premises anyway but still ... the bliss of the previous evening now all feels like a very distant dream. She woke up in the early hours of the morning and made me talk about my mother and my life. I told her things I have never told another human being. I laid my sins at her feet. The men I have killed, the way I rose to power and wealth, I hid nothing from her. After all she helped create the monster that I was. Let her dance with the devil she created.

I get to my feet refusing to acknowledge the ache in my heart that maybe I told her too much. Maybe this time she is truly gone.

The fear doesn't go away until I get into the bathroom and hear a slight sound coming from the shower stall. I take a few more steps and she comes into view. My eyes rove down her naked back all the way to her perfectly rounded ass. Such relief pours through my system I almost feel tearful. The way she looks! God, I want to grab her and make her mine all over again. Then it strikes me that she is behaving in a very curious manner.

"Liliana?"

Her head shoots up in alarm and she spins right around. She is so fast that I have to blink to reset my eyesight.

"What are you doing?" she asks defensively.

"What are *you* doing in my bathroom?" I ask.

She keeps her hands behind her body as though she is hiding something. "Nothing."

I look at her with amusement. "What are you hiding?"

I see her eyes dart to ascertain a likely escape route so I step subtly away to give her more space to dream of her escape. When she makes the mistake of taking it, my hand clamps around her waist. I pull her back against my body.

"Let me go," she cries, her head lowered as she scratches on my arm to release her. I look down to see my razor in her hand. Suddenly, I know what she is up to. Thoroughly entertained by her antics, I let her go then. She is too embarrassed to even meet my eyes.

"I'll be in my bathroom if you need me," she says nonchalantly.

"Where are you going with my razor?" I ask. "I need that to shave."

She is so shocked by my suggestion she whirls around to face me, her eyes wide. Finally, I am able to see the unfinished shave job on her sex. How I wished she had asked me to handle the task myself. It would have been the perfect morning chore.

"You can't use this?" she says in a scandalized tone.

"Why not?"

She looks horrified. "I've already used it to, you know? Hygiene Brand!"

I am sure she must be joking. "Liliana, a few hours ago your entire pussy was in my mouth and I was sucking it as if there was no tomorrow."

Like a magic trick, I watch Liliana turn a bright crimson. I don't know whether to laugh or to kiss her.

I throw my hands around her and grab her before she can run away again. Lifting her I put her on the bathroom counter.

"Let me go," she mewls, but her protest falls on deaf ears. I open her legs wide and slide my hand over the light stubble of her pussy before flicking on her bud, then slipping my fingers inside her. She gasps at the intrusion, but she is already wet and ready. In my head, I calculate how much time I have.

"You could have asked me to help you out," I whisper in her ear as her entire frame begins to tremble.

My fingers slip in and out.

"Stop talking about that and just fuck me," she cries with frustration.

"I would love to, but I have a deadly important meeting in half an hour. Well twenty minutes now." Her eyes fly open as she immediately stares into my eyes.

She stops my hand with both of hers. "Will you be okay?"

"When I say deadly I mean serious, Liliana, I'll be fine."

"You promised last night you will go straight."

"And I will. Step by step. There are certain codes in my life of business. If I walk out without fulfilling my responsibilities I'm a dead man."

She frowns. I increase the pace of my fingers in her and after a while she throws her head backwards. She is so close to coming I can feel it in the tightening of her pussy walls. I decide to finish myself off later, so I solely go after her climax. In no time she explodes on my hands.

I bring my fingers to my mouth and lick them clean of her taste, and she watches me, her gaze raw, and chest heaving. "I want us to fuck," she says.

I instantly release her, spanking her ass to send her on her way.

"Can't," I respond. "Meeting in fifteen."

"Brand." She pouts, but I gently push her out, and throwing my towel after her turn on the faucet.

I pull the door back open briefly however. "Leave it the way it is," I say with a nod of my chin at her sex. "I'll finish the job when I get back."

CHAPTER FORTY

Liliana

I do not see Brand before he leaves.

Once again, I am left alone in the house with nothing to do, and this time around with no one to speak to. I think of Pierre and hope that he is fine, and has not been scared too much by the previous evening. He got off easy, but I got off lucky.

I still cannot believe the time I have had with Brand.

For the first time he feels like a true lover to me. Last night was the sweetest night I have ever had in my life. My fear is for how it will all end. I really need to contact my father and soon. The longer I leave it the more worried and worked up he will become and the harder it will be to bring about a solution. Brand and my father are natural enemies, but I must somehow find a way for them to become friends.

I take a quick shower and even though it bothers me to be half shaven I leave the half-done job and go lie down on the couch downstairs. I am still quite sore. Last night I was able to ignore the pains in my back and arms from my fall and focus solely on Brand, but now that I am all alone, I can feel them throbbing. I smile when I think how easy it was to push aside my aches when I was with Brand.

When the doorbell rings around lunch time my heart jumps with the hope that it is Brand. It is not him. It is a food delivery service escorted by one of the guards. They come in and lay an extravagant array of dishes for me. I eat the food, read and watch some French TV. With the passing hours I start to fear that we will lose the comradeship of the previous evening.

Night falls again. Eventually, I fall asleep in front of the TV. I come awake the moment I hear Brand's SUV pull into the compound. The door clicks open and I sit up. I wait for his approach, anticipate and even pray for it, but when I hear his footsteps begin to climb up the stairs, my heart falls. Perhaps he doesn't know that I am here, I try to console myself, so I call out, "Brand."

He changes direction and comes to sit opposite me. He looks so incredibly guarded and wary it almost makes my heart fly out of my chest as I sit up. I know he must have had the same thoughts as me.

"How are you feeling?" he asks.

"I'm fine," I murmur.

His gaze roves over my body. "You don't feel any pain?"

I'm about to shake my head when I remember Pierre's advice about breaking arms and legs. "Just on my right hand," I reply demurely.

His brows furrow in concern. Coming closer he takes my

hand in his to inspect it, and I make sure to wince properly when he presses on the part that only remotely hurts.

"Let's go for a check-up," he says and starts to rise to his feet, but I immediately grab onto him to sit back down.

"Actually, it feels a bit better now," I say. "I'm sure it will be fine in a couple of days. I hate hospitals."

He nods slowly. "Alright then, let me know how it feels tomorrow."

I move even closer to him and trap him between my legs. He gazes at my stretch of long limbs and my hands holding on lightly to his jacket.

Lowering my eyes I speak in the softest voice I have. "I want something."

"What is it?" he asks, and my heart stutters in excitement. The door to the house opens then and I look up to see the arrival of his main guard, however when I return my gaze back to Brand I see his eyes fully on me. The guy turns around and goes back out of the room.

"Go on," he says. Our faces are so close to each other his eyes are like black wells that I can drown in and his breath is tickling my face, and his scent of wood and musk is slowly intoxicating me.

"I want us to go on a date."

He blinks.

"You know, like a real date. I get dressed up and we go out to eat. Like in *Pretty Woman*."

He smiles. "Are you such a child that you think real life is like a movie?"

"No, but I love that movie. Both Mum and me like to watch it together. We do the whole business with popcorn, hotdogs and bags of jelly beans."

The mention of my mother and my life with my family makes him frown.

Shit. Trust me to go ruin the mood. I look at him from under my lashes. "You nearly came home to me naked but for one of your ties knotted around my neck."

His eyes gleam. "What stopped you?"

"Couldn't find the right tie," I joke.

He sighs. It is clear that he is preoccupied with something else. "Yes, I'll take you on a date, Liliana Eden."

"Thank you," I say to him and I want to kiss him so badly, but it doesn't seem right. He seems sad somehow. Perhaps his meetings didn't go well. All my life I have never seen my father look sad. No matter what happens at work, he always has a smile full of sunshine for my mum.

Brand drags his gaze away from mine and towards his door. "What is it?"

"Phone call, boss," the guard standing outside the door says.

Brand turns back to me. "Have you eaten?"

I nod.

"Go upstairs then," he says softly.

I jump up with a bright smile. "Okay." I hurry up the stairs, my heart pounding hard. I asked him out on a date and he said yes! I lean against the wall, a stupid grin on my face. Alright what am I to do now? He said go upstairs but that can mean either my room or his. I know I want to be with him tonight. I look at the two doors and summon up the courage to go into his room.

The worst he can do is kick me out.

As I sit on his bed, the thought occurs to me that kicking me out might be a little harder to do if I am already asleep. So I strip, pulling off my khaki shorts and t-shirt till I am dressed only in my underwear. I take off my bra for double effect and slide underneath the covers. Then I shut my eyes and practice controlling my breathing to a steady rhythm. About half an hour later when I am almost truly asleep I hear him come into the room.

It brings me instantly awake and I quickly control my breathing to pull off my pretense of being asleep. If he is anything like my father as I suspect, faking sleep is not something that I can even dream of getting away with. I hear him stop for a little bit and wonder whether he will think I am taking liberties and ask me to leave, but he only heads towards the bathroom. A few minutes later he returns and the mattress next to me compresses.

He lies next to me, but he doesn't try to pull me to him and curl up against me. My real acting begins then. I wait a little while, then keeping my eyes shut, I combine a little provocative moaning sound with a little maneuvering and some light flailing of my arms. Suddenly, I am right next to him. This is enough. I'm close enough that I can feel his warmth. Anymore and it will be too obvious.

"You are a little minx, aren't you?" Brand says in the dark.

My heart almost stops. I consider pretending I don't know what he is talking about, but what's the point? "I missed you all day," I whisper.

"So did I, Liliana. So did I," he says as he pulls me into his arms. He makes love to me in a way he has never done. There is something desperate about the silent, vicious thrusts. As if this is our last time, or as if he just can't get enough of me.

CHAPTER FORTY-ONE

Liliana

I fall asleep with him inside me, and wake up still spooned against Brand. His head is resting in the cradle of my neck. One of his arms is wrapped around my chest, while the other is under my pillow.

His breathing is steady and I know that he is still asleep. When I try to move, Brand pulls me even closer. For the next few minutes I just lay there savoring the unbeatable feeling of being in his arms. I know the moment he comes awake. Without a word he lets go of me, rises to his feet, and gets out of bed. I turn to see him leave, dressed in only a pair of dark briefs and instantly I go after him.

A few seconds later I follow him and find him leaning against the counter, his head lowered and eyes shut. I lean against the door and watch him curiously. My hair is long enough to cover my breasts, so I don't feel too self-conscious standing before him naked.

The movement alerts him to my presence and he glances at me through the mirror.

"Are you all right?" I ask.

He straightens and nods. "Yeah." Then he retrieves a can of shaving cream and rubs it over his lower face. Taking a deep breath, I head towards him and stop behind his broad, strong back. I am quite short compared to Brand I realize with some surprise. I barely reach his shoulders. Sliding my arm around his waist, I press my chest to his back and start to trace patterns down his skin as I speak.

"I want to shave you today," I whisper.

He goes very still. The seconds go by without any reaction from him. Then he catches my wrists and begins to pull my arms away from his waist. I feel the tears of disappointment sting my eyes. It's always one step forward and two back with him. To my surprise, though, he turns around lifts me up and places me on the counter. I gaze up at him with a mixture of adoration and surprise as he positions himself between my legs and hands me the razor.

"Be careful," he says to me, and shuts his eyes.

His lashes are long, very long, I realize. The luxuriously thick hairs brush his cheeks. His jaw is strong, and his hair is slicked away from his face. *Damn he is handsome*. I want to kiss him, but his face is already covered in shaving cream so I lean down and begin to press kisses along his shoulders.

It makes him laugh. He leans slightly away from me. "I thought you wanted to shave me," he says.

I want him so much I can barely speak. "You should have fucked me before you got out of bed," I say quietly, "now I think my hands are too shaky to do a good job."

His shining eyes darken with desire as his head lowers to take my breasts in my mouth. He sucks on the mounds, his hand giving me a caress sweet enough to melt stone. He traces kisses down my skin, and then down my belly towards my sex. Before he can go all the way down I pull him back up. "I don't want shaving cream all the way there, look what you've done already." We both glance down at the trails of white suds he has left down my body. His smile makes it hard to breathe.

"You need some of it down there, anyway," he says, "have you forgotten I'm meant to shave you too?"

My face turns red and it makes him laugh out loud. The sound is boisterous and beautiful. I stare at him.

"You're so fucking adorable when you blush," he says.

"I wonder what would make you blush."

"Killers don't blush, Princess."

I sober up instantly and the mood between us changes. I look deep into his eyes. "I don't care what you did in the past. I am only interested in the present and the future."

"You think we have a future together, Princess?"

"Yes, I think so. I know I can convince my father. My mother says my father has not said no to me since I was two years old."

He smiles sadly. "Yeah, I bet he hasn't. Nobody's said no to you, have they Princess?"

"You have."

"No, I fucking haven't. You've got me all twisted around your little finger."

"Well, you've got me all twisted around your big dick."

He laughs. "Okay. You win. Now, why don't you shave me first then I'll do you, and we can finish this off in the shower."

"Sounds good," I say to him and with my legs pull him back towards me and pick up the razor.

"Be careful," he warns.

"Don't be such a little coward. I'm not going to hurt you."

"I know," he says, "but your hand still hurts, doesn't it?"

I look into his eyes, "It does, but not enough for me to slip." There might be something in Pierre's advice. With a secret smile at his concern I begin to shave away at his slight stubble.

"You're surprisingly good at this," he comments.

"I'm my father's daughter–" I immediately stop at the dangerous topic, and just in time to see his gaze drop from mine. He doesn't urge me to go on, and neither do I. The fear is almost as intense as the excitement. It seems that neither of us can quite get enough of our new-found harmony, but at the same time it almost seems as though we're both just waiting for it to break, for whatever miracle that has caused this camaraderie between us to just shatter into a million pieces.

With my hands on his shoulder to keep him in place, I carry on moving the razor up and down his face slowly. As more skin is exposed I can't help but notice how baby soft and smooth it is.

I ask him about it and his reply is simple. "I have no idea. I just use whatever Lindy puts in my bathroom."

His casual careless answer makes me smile. Of course, he doesn't give a shit what cream he puts on his face. Soon I am completely done. I put the shaving stick down. Before I can reach for a towel to wipe his face, he grabs my thighs.

"Put your arms around my neck," he says, and I immediately do as instructed. He pulls my ass forward and pushes on my chest so I am leaning against the mirror.

Brand spreads my legs apart.

"It might be a bit uncomfortable for you in a few days," I mumble shyly. "I usually use something else."

Brand pumps shaving cream unto his hands and begins to slather it all over my sex, his eyes full of concentration. "I'll take you any way I can get you."

At his words, I am able to relax as he takes the razor gently in and out of my crevices, his hands as steady as I'd expect from a man like him. When he is finished he wipes me clean.

"There. Freshly shaven and ready to be fucked."

Picking me up he takes me into the shower stall and there, he kisses me so passionately I just plain give up on the notion of standing on my own two feet. I cling to his neck, my eyes gazing into his as he washes me with soap, his fingers teasing between the lips of my sex.

"Are you cleaning me up or trying to get me dirty again?" I gasp.

The corner of his mouth slightly tilts up in a sexy smirk just before he takes my lips. I hold on for dear life, completely lost to the man and the torment of his charm.

Somehow we manage to leave the bathroom after an hour and once again I am sat on the counter as Brand dries me up. My stratagem is simple. A pout and a soft purr of '*my arm hurts*' and I get taken care of like a baby. How I wish Pierre is still around just so I can give him a big hug for his "advice". I don't even dare mention him, lest I trigger Brand. I don't want to risk my current state of euphoric bliss. Once I am bone dry and feeling like a cat that got the cream I pick up his lotion and begin to rub the light liquid all over his perfect face.

"I'm jealous of your skin," I say to him, turning to the bottle and reading the fine print. "What is this that Lindy has bought for you? Woah! Korean snail essence?"

He smiles. "Do you know I couldn't read or write until I met Lindy."

I turn to look at him. "You really owe a lot to that woman, don't you?"

He nods slowly. "Yeah. I don't know what I would have become without her."

I take his drier from him and begin to blow dry his hair. Our time together is quiet and we are both still mindful of straying too far into forbidden topics, but it is oh, so wonderful.

I am worried though about the time he has spent with me. "Won't you be leaving the house today?" I ask as casually as I can.

"Later on," he says to me and that is a good enough answer.

"I'll make you breakfast then," I say to him.

He instantly shuts me down. "No need, I'll order something in."

"Oh," I say and watch as he pulls on his pants. I'm in a towel and about to head to my room to get changed, but just before I pull the door open, I change my mind, and decide to be bold. "I'm making you breakfast, Brand Vaughan," I say to him. "Nothing in this world beats my blueberry pancakes so you better be damned psyched to try it out."

He is startled at my sudden outburst, and for a few moments I am not sure if my move was smart or just plain overbearing so I sheepishly add, "You will be forever changed. I swear it."

Brand nods, as a small smile plays on his lips.

Trying to control the warmth swelling in my heart, I exit the room and hurry to get changed. Brand unsettles me. I am not sure what Brand's true personality is. He used to be cruel and sardonic, but now it seems as though he is calmly watching it all, watching me … but for what or why I am not certain.

CHAPTER FORTY-TWO

Brand

9 years earlier

For almost two horrendous weeks I was taken to other stately houses for 'parties' where other monsters had the same ideas for lubrication.

Then I realized how I could escape.

When Havant came down with his taser he saw me lying prone in bed. He fired his gun at me and saw me jerking around on the bed. When he was certain I was incapacitated he came in. Imagine his shock when I attacked him from behind.

I was hiding behind the door. The person on the bed was a dummy I had made using my clothes and the mattress filling. I had connected it to a piece of wood I had broken off the bed so I could jerk the dummy around from behind the door.

I had waited four hours for the bastard to come down.

Naked and almost blue with cold I was almost out of my

mind with fear and rage. I kicked the shit out of that low life. He was a real coward. He pissed and shat himself. Once he was unconscious I got dressed and made my way to the first floor. When I found no one there I ran as far away as I could from his hellhole.

I began to live on the streets. I'd beg at the train station and sleep in the dumpster at night. A couple of times I got robbed and once beaten up by a gang of thugs, but then I found out about this place you could go to for a hot meal. There were a lot of do-gooders there and a lot of unwashed drunks, but that was also where I met Lindy.

Two weeks after moving in with Lindy, a man approached me in the street. He said he needed a runner. Nothing dangerous. Mostly carrying money from one club to another. Someone to do little things. Someone under-aged who the authorities would go easy on.

After a week, he offered to send me to school. He told me to be a criminal I needed to have an appetite for violence. Pain, he said, made a man weak and I had too much pain inside. Long story short, he didn't think I had it in me.

Shit! I was surprised. He was actually offering me to go straight. I thought of his generous offer, but I decided not to take it. I didn't want to become another tax paying cog in the machinery.

No, I wanted to be as rich as Jake Eden. I started hanging around with other young, ambitious gangsters, but I had something they didn't. Raw, undiluted anger. After what those men had done to me I took to violence like a duck takes to water. The need for revenge was like a disease in my blood. I went back to Havant's house and torched it. The next day Lindy read the newspapers and told me that a man had died in the blaze. I would have dearly loved to pay a visit to some of those sick men who abused me, but I was always taken in the back of vans and did not know how to return to those great houses.

Just once I saw one of them. The creep was with his wife and kid. She was blonde and so up her ass, I wanted to go up to her and tell her what her husband did for kicks when she was not around.

I walked up to him and pretended to spill my cup of coffee on him. He jumped up furiously, cursing and ready to lash out. Then he looked into my eyes and suddenly he went as white as a sheet. He fell back in his chair and mumbled his apologies.

I smiled very slowly.

I got him a job feeding the fishes at the bottom of the Thames. But before that I taught him all about lubrication.

Yeah, well, so goes life. I never saw my father again. He died of a broken heart in prison, but my rise as a gangster was nothing short of meteoric.

CHAPTER FORTY-THREE

Liliana

*A*s I sprint down the stairs, I can see him already at the bottom of the stairs on his phone. He has on dark slacks, and a sky-blue jumper and it makes him look so elegantly sexy that I feel a rush of pride. That's my man there! As I reach the last rung of the staircase, I spread out my arms and jump straight at him.

To his credit he reacts fast. Catching me while still keeping his phone in his hand. Even so my jump is so sudden and unexpected he staggers a few steps backwards, his back hitting the door. I feel like an overly exuberant sibling in the arms of an incredibly patient brother, but I can see that he has no experience being playful.

He is staring straight into my eyes with an odd expression.

"Straight to the kitchen, young man," I command in an impervious voice.

Shaking his head at my silliness, he indulges my request. Putting me on my feet he goes to the table and takes another incoming phone call. I head over to the fridge and start gathering all the ingredients I'll need. When I glance at him, I see him watching me intently as he listens to the speaker on the other end of his phone.

While he takes out a pad and pen and starts scribbling down notes I make a start on the big breakfast I'd planned to impress him with. When Brand rounds up his call, he comes over and takes the can of baked beans I was about to open and starts to do it for me, saying, "You shouldn't be straining your hand."

Ah yes, my hand. Pierre wouldn't approve, but I go behind him and slide my arms around his waist. "Actually, my hand doesn't hurt anymore."

"No?"

"No," I say, reveling in his warmth. I have to admit my interest in cooking has diminished somewhat since I put my cheek on his back.

"Let me see your hand," he says.

I allow him to raise my wrist and inspect it. "See, it's all better."

"Hmmm ...While I am here I might as well make myself useful. What do you need help with?"

I look towards the onions with which I plan to make an omlette.

"Want to help me chop those?"

"Onions?" he says with a smile.

I grin tauntingly. "Would you like to do something a bit ... easier?"

He pulls up the sleeves of his sweater and reaches for a knife and I am left just staring after him still wondering if I am dreaming. When did we become lovers who could tease each other? He notes my surprise, and stops over to kiss me. It is a slow, sweet job that shoots a painful ache of pleasure straight to my core.

Poor Brand. Tears pour down his eyes, but he won't give up. He places a bowl of chopped onions in front of me. "What next?"

I get him to measure out the ingredients for my pancake batter and we settle into an efficient partnership. It is when I'm behind the counter, whisking the bowl of eggs that Brand comes behind me. With his hands on my hips he presses my ass into his groin. He is aroused, painfully so, and so am I. I slowly grind myself against him as his lips drag kisses along the side of my neck.

Vaguely I note that I'm losing the steady rhythm with the whisk, but as he continues I don't even realize when it falls to the ground. Brand ignores it also. Slipping his hands into my shirt he takes hold of my breasts. By now my breathing is labored. I spread my legs apart and he slips his hand between my thighs and runs his fingers along my already soaking wet slit.

"No underwear?" he asks.

"Uh ... I didn't think it would be necessary."

"Great call."

Reaching behind me I undo his slacks and he caresses my pussy in rapid circular motions. I have to say, he gets me off in record time. Before I can recover fully I feel the hard thick head of his cock nudging at the lips of my sex.

A wild giggle escapes my lips as he strokes it against me. My back is already arched and ready so the moment he slams the thick shaft into me my grip on the edge of the counter is the only thing holding me up. With a hand under my thigh, he gently lifts my leg up, then begins to drill into me.

He moves in a fast, hard rhythm I have trouble keeping up with. Hell, he fucks me till I am nearly crippled. Wc come together. My scream echoes loudly around the still room.

Brand tucks his dick back into his trousers. "Order in?" he asks.

I shrug and nod.

CHAPTER FORTY-FOUR

Brand

*M*y eyes are supposed to be on my accountant's reports before me, but the chair is angled just enough that I have a decent view of Liliana lying on the couch lost in a book.

Her presence calms me. I look forward to it. I look at her now and I feel no anger. When I hear her turn a page I am unable to stop myself from turning to watch her. I cannot stop watching her ... and wanting her.

But my heart is troubled.

I know it will be war with her father. There is no way he is going to roll over and let me keep her. I don't know how I will find a solution to this problem. I don't want to hurt him because I know it will hurt her and I don't want to hurt her or risk losing her again. But if I don't destroy him, he will destroy me. I used to hate him so much. I was angry with him.

I've been angry for so long. There was so much to be angry at, and for a very long while that pain and anger was all I had.

It kept me strong. It motivated me, but for now, just in these few days, I do not want to be angry. I want to enjoy the surprising peace and wholeness that I find with Liliana.

I always wondered why I could never let her go, why I could never get her off my mind. I was sure it was at my need to avenge my parents, but perhaps that was just a tiny bit of it. Perhaps there was more that the world wanted to pull my attention to.

Perhaps it is because she and I share the same soul. We are like two pieces that cannot be parted.

She looks up from her book and it's too late for me to look away. I am caught red-handed, staring at her like a lovesick fool. But she stares right back. Then softly, kindly, she smiles at me, and I feel my chest tighten so much that it is hard to breathe.

CHAPTER FORTY-FIVE

Liliana

https://www.youtube.com/watch?v=Sv6dMFF_yts

*I*t is our first date together. I stand in front of Brand in my dress and make up. He stares at me as if he can't believe his eyes.

I smile up at him. He is dressed like a Mafia don, in a black silk shirt and black trousers. I like that he looks so dangerous and dark, but one day, I will throw away all his black silk shirts. One day he will be totally legit, like my father and all my uncles. My father used to say only a fool or a man without choices would be a criminal longer than he needed to because in the end all criminals end up behind bars if they don't come to a nasty end before that.

"Well what do you think?" I ask, twirling around.

"You look beautiful," he breathes.

"Are you sure I've got enough blusher on?"

"You don't need any more color." Amusement makes his eyes twinkle. "But if you do I'll just finger you under the table. Your entire face will turn pink."

"Promises, promises."

He raises an eyebrow. "You think I won't do it."

I wrinkle my nose. "I'm counting on you to do it."

We get into his SUV. Mark is driving, but it is too quiet between us. I am usually quite talkative, but between us silence usually means that unquiet thoughts have taken control.

I look down to see his hand resting on the seat so I place mine softly on his. Moving closer to him I nibble along his jawline. It has two effects. It makes him smile, and it brings Mark's surprised gaze through the rearview mirror. He immediately returns his eye to the road while I return mine to Brand who slips his hand around my waist to pull me closer.

I lean up to whisper into his ear. "Will Mark mind if we have a quick rehearsal of what you intend to do to me at the restaurant?"

His laughter fills the car in an instant. Brand places a soft kiss on my forehead and it warms me all over. "He might not, but I very much will."

The restaurant is in the city and we have to drive out for almost an hour to get to it. It is a private club. Very expensive and very snooty. The walls seem to be carved out in gold moldings and accentuated by cupids and murals and the chairs are a striking electric blue. The entire room is candle lit, and combined with the low chatter of other patrons and with its soft warmth, it is the perfect setting for a romantic dinner.

We are seated opposite each other, but the arrangement is quite regal, so we are not as close to each other as I'd hoped. The moment the waiter takes his leave with our order, I lightly kick Brand's legs under the table.

"You made me a promise," I complain.

His smile is torturously suggestive. "Oh, don't worry. I'll take you somewhere after this." The glint in his eyes and the promise are more than enough to take me through our dinner.

The waiters bring little teaser foods topped with feather soft cream. I take the liberty of tapping a dot on Brand's nose. His smile lights up the whole room. Before he can clean it off I stop him and rise to my feet.

It would be too much of a stretch to lean over and take it off the way I want to so I rise with the excuse of going to the Ladies. I circle the table and lean down as though I want to whisper into his ear. My lips cover the tip of his nose for a brief second before I scurry away.

His laughter accompanies me as I make my way towards the bathroom.

CHAPTER FORTY-SIX

Brand

*T*here is no one watching Liliana ... and she is fully aware of this.

There is still a smile on my face as I follow her progress towards the toilets, her velvety, high-slit dress hugging every curve of her beautiful body, until she disappears out of sight.

Then I look down at my hand. It is tightly clenched. How much of her heart is truly mine? Why I should feel anxious is beyond me? She could have run away that night with Pierre. She didn't. I watch the hallway leading to the bathroom, intently, waiting ... and too afraid to think of the possibility that she has made a fool of me. Like she did before.

The seconds tick away and then the minutes.

I await Liliana with a kind of sick dread ... and every person that emerges from the shadows of the hallways brings hope to my heart until it is revealed that she is not the one.

My gaze turns towards the view beyond of the hills above the Côte d'Azur. I don't know why I brought her here. It was a stupid idea. All she has to do is get out of the front door and slip into a Metro. The nearest metro is like fifty meters away from this restaurant. I think of her laughing. I think of us in bed. Her skin warm and soft. Suddenly, I can bear it no more. I can't let her go. I stand and a waiter appears at my side to ask if there is anything wrong. Ignoring him I take a step forward. My mouth feels dry. I miscalculated.

Then I see her coming towards me.

My mouth opens and air rushes out of it. She comes up to me, a frown on her face. "What's the matter? You look pale."

I shake my head. "Nothing is the matter."

I watch as Liliana takes her seat in front of me, a strained smile on her face. "Are you sure you are all right?"

I pick up my glass of Irish whisky and knock it back.

She returned. *She returned to me.*

The food arrives with a great deal of fuss and fanfare.

"Bon appetite," I say.

She tucks her hair behind her ears nervously and picks up her fork.

"We're returning tomorrow," I say to her.

All we hear is the clinking of cutleries in the background and the low buzz of chatter from the other dining couples in the restaurant.

She puts her fork down, picks up her glass of wine, and takes a large swallow. "Okay. How are we going to be when we return?"

"I don't know, Liliana."

"What is going to happen when we get back?"

Until that moment, my heart was undecided. But as I look at her my response comes. "I don't know what is going to happen, but I can't let you go."

Tears shimmer in her eyes. "You have to let me go back to my father and talk to him. That is the only way this will work."

"I can't take the chance. You are mine now. I don't recognize his authority over you."

"Please. You have to let me go to my family. My father loves me. He wants me to be happy."

"Yeah, like he did when he fired my dad just because I kissed you?" I ask coldly.

CHAPTER FORTY-SEVEN

Liliana

*H*e doesn't take me to a place where he had promised to make me climax under a table. Instead we go back to the farmhouse and sit at the kitchen table. As long as I live I will never forget this night. Under the overhead lamp his face is craggy and his eyes bleak. We drink whisky straight from the bottle and we talk.

Ah, how we talk.

There is so much to say. So much to know. Sometimes there are tears in our eyes. He finds out I think gray pitt bulls are absolutely adorable and I find out about the brutality of men in grand stately homes. It makes my hands tremble with fury and my heart break for that dark-haired proud boy who kissed me. How dare they do that to a kid? As he talks about them the rage comes back.

"I saw one of them in the newspapers once. Lord Hetherington was apparently a respected member of the House of Lords and a very eminent judge who believed the age of consent should be reduced. I heard he cried and sniveled like a fucking coward for a very long time before he died."

I don't blame him for executing the judge. I would have done it myself. People like that shouldn't exist. Who knows how many other boys have been taken, abused, and murdered?

I take sips from the bottle and he takes gulps. By the time we are halfway down the second bottle he is very drunk. I want to tell him I love him, but the words stick in my throat. Love seems like such a tame word. I mean, I love ice cream, but what I feel for Brand is like the ocean, wide, deep, endless, unfathomable. After everything that has happened between us I would go to the ends of the earth for him, give up my life for him.

I watch as his movements become relaxed, his speech slurring slightly, and his head starts to droop.

"Should we go to bed?" I ask.

He looks up at me. "I'm not letting you go, Liliana."

"I know. I don't want you to let me go."

"Just so you know. I'll die before I fuckin' give you up."

"Nobody is going to die," I say firmly.

He looks sad and lost. "I'm afraid you don't know your father very well. You might have to choose between him and me."

I stand so suddenly the wooden chair crashes to the stone floor. "Don't say that. My father will never do anything to hurt me. If he hurts you he hurts me. And I know you will never hurt him because if you hurt him you hurt me."

"There is too much water under the bridge now for that. Too much hatred."

"Forgive me," I say. "Forgive my father, and most importantly forgive yourself. That is the only way any of us can move beyond this."

"Until I took you as my pawn I could blame you. Pretend it was all your fault, but now that Band Aid has been ripped off. The cancer was me. It was my fault all along. I caused it all." He pauses before crying out in anguish. "I can't forgive myself."

"Until when?" I ask passionately. "Until when will you think this way? Until something happens to me, or to my father? Or until something happens to you, and you look back to regret why you were so unmerciful to yourself you never allowed yourself to be happy. That you never set yourself free. How would your parents feel watching all of this?"

His eyes darken, and his face becomes chillingly cold suddenly. "Don't mention them."

"I'm sorry," I say instantly. The last thing I want to do is push him away.

He looks exhausted and pale suddenly. "No, you have nothing to be sorry for. It's not your fault. Let's go to bed, Princess."

We stagger upstairs. There is a full moon outside and with the snow on the ground his bedroom is full of blue light. He lands on the bed on his back and I begin to undress him.

"Are we going to fuck?" he asks.

I chuckle. "Somehow I don't think so."

"Why? Don't you want to?"

"Um ... you might have trouble getting it up."

"I never have trouble getting it up, Princess. Not where

you're concerned," he replies, but his eyelids are already clos-
ing. Gently, I take off his shirt and his trousers. It is while I
am undressing him that I see the tattoo I had seen it before.
A knife with an intricately carved handle, but what I had not
noticed previously were the letters on the blade.

Liliana

I run my fingers along my name. His skin is silky and warm. I
feel tears blur my eyes. Oh, how he has suffered because of
one careless action. All sensations of sleep have disappeared
so I pull a chair by his side and I sit by him. I have never
watched someone have a more troubled sleep. His movements thoroughly restless as though no position seems good
enough, while his breathing pattern is continuously irregular,
as though he is either fighting dragons in his dreams, or he's
just tormented. His face is constantly frowning and sometimes he makes little sounds. Once he calls my name.

My heart twists as I watch him, and although I do not want
to wake him up, I cannot just sit by and watch any longer.
Rising from the chair I get into bed with him. I spoon him
with my front to his back and placing my hand on his heart I
rest my cheek in the crook of his neck.

That is when I hear him take his first deep breath. As the
minutes pass he falls in a deeper slumber. A proper one where
he stops moving restlessly, his breathing becomes even, and
he turns only once to pull me into his arms. It makes me
certain that he can sense my presence.

He wraps his hand around me and like a child I lay my head
against his chest. We fall asleep that way. I'm awakened a few
hours later, by Brand untangling himself from me. The

moment I open my eyes I see him staring around, disoriented, wondering at his position.

"What is it?" I whisper.

"I don't know. I think something is wrong."

"It's okay. It's nothing," I say, just as the sound of something
crashing to the floor downstairs tears through the still air.

CHAPTER FORTY-EIGHT
Liliana

https://www.youtube.com/watch?v=pLobxewHbjo
Now we are Free

I freeze, but Brand jackknives out of bed and starts putting on his pants. His eyes are astonishingly shiny and alert. His cellphone starts to vibrate. He immediately picks it up. In the deathly silence I can hear Mark's voice come through, rapid and tense.

"We are being attacked. Eden is here."

"How many down?" Brand barks as he takes out his gun.

"I don't know, but Khalid is out," Mark says.

"I'm coming," he says and kills the line. He turns to me. I'm so shocked I have not moved an inch. "Stay here. Whatever happens don't come out."

I sit up. "No, wait, Brand."

"I mean it, Liliana. This is between me and your dad. Don't come out." He starts walking away and all I can do is just stare at his naked back. At the door he turns back and looks at me. Then he says the words that electrify me. "I love you, Liliana. I always have and I always will. If I never see you again, remember that."

Then he is gone. I jump out of bed and run to the door just as he locks it from outside. Instead of trying to bang it I run to the window. There is a tree branch close to the window and it looks like it could handle my weight. Without thinking of the consequences or looking down at the ground below I get on the branch. I exhale and my breath becomes clouds of mist in front of me.

It is freezing cold, but like a little monkey I quickly climb down the tree and get to the front door. It is wide open. As I get to the hallway I see my Dad. He has a gun pointed at Brand and Brand has his gun trained on Dad.

Oh, Jesus Christ.

"Tell your men to stand down," my father is saying. "We're not here to make trouble, I'm here only to take my daughter back." His eyes are fierce and cold. I have never seen him like that. He looks like a stranger. My great-grandmother on my mother's side was Chinese, and she used to teach me a lot of proverbs when I was small. One of them was: human beings are full of secrets. You can eat salt with a person for seven years and never know them. That is what I felt watching my father at that moment.

Brand laughs. "You mean you're not here for revenge. You don't want to see me dead. I kidnapped your daughter. I made a fool of the great Jake Eden."

I rush into the room. "Dad," I call.

My father looks at me and I see a flash of something I recognize. It is what I have seen all my life. Love. "Get out, Liliana" he says.

"No," I say coming further into the room. "I'm not a child. I want to have my say in this."

"Get out, Liliana," Brand says.

"No." I take another step closer to Brand. I know Brand will never fire on my dad, but I saw it in my dad's eyes that he would be more than willing to kill Brand.

"Liliana," my father calls, his voice is harsh. "This is an order and not up for discussion. Go back out. *Now*. This is between Brand and me."

"No, Dad, this is not between just you and Brand. This involves me too. Brand is John the gardener's son, Dad. Remember him? I got him fired. It was my fault. It was just an innocent kiss. I should never have come crying to you. I made it sound worse than what it was. Because of us something terrible happened to Brand after that, Dad."

My father keeps his aim steady on Brand.

"Dad, if you hurt Brand, I will never be able to live normally again. I will feel guilty for ever. Is that what you want for me? Please, Dad. I've forgiven him for kidnapping me. You just have to forgive him too. He didn't mistreat me. He wasn't cruel or anything like that. He just made a mistake the same way I made a mistake. Just look at me, Dad."

Then, before my dad can respond, a freaky thing happens, one of Brand's men bursts through the door with a gun in his hand. He comes through with such momentum, he slams into the kitchen table, and dislodges a bullet. It should have just made a hole in the ceiling, but it ricochets off a metal pipe and tears into the flesh of my stomach.

The sensation of being shot is like having a white-hot poker in your flesh. The pain is unimaginable. I scream and the impact of the bullet throws me to the ground.

After that everything seems to happen in slow motion. Other men run in. The panic and confusion is surreal. Brand forgets my dad, flings his gun to the ground and runs towards me. His face is stricken and white as a sheet. He lifts my upper body on to his lap. He is so shocked he can't even speak. My Dad on the other hand does not come to him. He is on the phone straight away to call the helicopter to get to the farm-house. As soon as that call is over he contacts the best surgeon in London whom he has apparently already flown down in his private jet to be on standby. He even seems to know which hospital I will be taken to.

I start to feel woozy. I call my Dad. Ignoring Brand, he crouches in front of me. "Help is on its way. You're going to be just fine," he says calmly.

I can feel the blood pouring out of me. "Am I going to die?"

Brand tightens his hold on me. "No, you're not going to die. I won't let you die."

"Dad, you know how much I hate to see blood, right?"

He touches my hair. "Don't look down, darling. Just don't look down. Everything is going to be fine." When he presses his lips together I see the skin around his mouth is white.

I look into my father's eyes. "When I'm out, don't hurt him, Dad. I love him. I've always loved him."

My father's eyes widen with shock. "He's a criminal, Liliana."

"He can change," I whisper. I can feel the pain receding.

"Criminals don't change their spots," he says harshly.

I start to feel woozy. "Dad, remember when you told me the story of the prostitute and the monk?"

He stares at me. "I didn't think you actually listened to any of my stories."

"I did. Am I the monk or the prostitute?"

Tears come into his eyes. "Okay, Liliana. Okay. I trust you."

"I'm just going to sleep for bit. Don't you two fight now."

"No, no sleeping," Dad booms. "You must stay awake, darling."

"Talk to me, babe," Brand says. I look into his eyes. The edges of my vision are getting blurred, but they never completely blur because between Brand and my dad, I never get to sleep until we arrive at the hospital.

CHAPTER FORTY-NINE

Brand

I feel like a man broken. I can see Liliana's father striding up and down the small waiting room floor making calls, arranging things, reassuring his family, talking to other professionals in their field about Liliana's subsequent care, but I can't even move. For the first time in my life I feel completely helpless. I look again at my hands in surprise. They are still shaking. Her blood is still on them.

I know she will make it, but the shock of seeing her being shot still makes me feel nauseous. My God, she could have died. My God, I could have lost her. I swallow hard and stand. Jake Eden immediately turns his head in my direction. For the longest time we stare at each other.

"What do you want?" I growl finally. I'm not giving Liliana up. Not for him. Not for anyone.

His expression is hard. "You have something of mine. Where is it?"

I know instantly he is talking about his ring. "It's in England. At my home."

"I'm sending someone to your house now. Will you arrange for it to be handed to them?"

I nod slowly. "Yeah. I can do that."

"Sit down. We might as well get this over with."

I immediately become defensive. Every sinew in my body hardens. I know he is going to try to convince me to give up Liliana. "What?"

He sits down. "I want to apologize."

Suspicious of his real intentions I take a seat opposite him and cross my arms over my chest. "You do?"

"Yes, my apology to you is long overdue. However, over the years I have ensured that I continually made up for the losses that I cost you."

My eyes widen. "What?"

He shrugs. "You're twenty-four and insanely wealthy. Do you think that it is all by your own doing? The business you are in was how I began my career. I know it like the back of my hand. Have you never wondered why it was so easy for you to break in, or did you just think it was pure luck?"

"I ..."

"It is also a bloody path, and yet you seem to have been shielded from most of the turf wars that you should have fought by now. There are numerous times you should have even lost your life. Have you never wondered why it has been so easy for you?"

The truth in his words begins to dawn on me. My path has been rocky, but not as bloody as it should have been. "What the fuck are you really saying?"

His next words shock the life out of me. My head starts pounding. I stare at him in astonishment.

He leans his wide frame back on the back of the chair. "I am that person you were always so keen to meet, Brand. I am Victor Maeterlinck."

"What the ...? You are Victor Maeterlinck?" I repeat in disbelief. Victor Maeterlinck was a legend and a mystery. No one had ever met him. He was rumored to be a Belgian living in Monaco. Some said he was a fat, round thing who incessantly smoked cigars, others said he was six foot six. He was also my boss. Over the years he had passed a lot of big jobs to me through intermediaries.

He nods.

I shake my head in disbelief. "All these years I've actually been working for you."

"Yes, life is a funny old thing. After I got married I knew things had to change and I'd always liked the idea of running an invisible empire. So much harder to unravel and deniability is such a good thing."

I stare at him. The irony was not lost on me. All these years I've spent hating Jake Eden and I was working for him! "Does Liliana know?"

"Of course not. No one knows." He moves closer to me. "It's a secret, Brand. And now you're in on it too."

I feel a flare of pride. Jake had trusted me his big secret. "Why did you do all this for me?"

He shrugs again. "It was my way of saying sorry. I fired your Dad in a fit of temper, but when I cooled down I knew I had done the wrong thing. Especially when news of your mother's death filtered back to me. Your father was a good man and a good employee so I looked for him, but he died in prison exactly a week after he went in. What else was I to do but take over the job of being your father? Remember that first offer you had to go straight. To have your education paid for. That was me. But you refused."

"Yes," I look into his eyes. "I wanted to be like you."

"After that I made it my business to protect you," he says, "and connected you. Remember Marcus? He met you in Leicester and he introduced you to this world. It wasn't an accident. I sent him to you too. He nurtured you on my behalf. However, from now on and based on what you have done to my daughter, I consider us both even. My daughter thinks she is in love with you, but we will see. I am hoping it is an infatuation."

At that moment, a doctor enters the room and Jake immediately walks up to him. "How is she?" he asks.

The doctor smiles. It is clear they are old friends. "She'll be just fine, Jake." He turns to me. "Are you Brand?"

I nod.

"She's called your name a couple of times."

Tears fill my eyes. Never have I been so overwhelmed and confused all at once, but if there are any lessons I have learned from life is that everything happens for a reason. Fate put her in front of me to tempt me. And now Fate has brought her back to me. I would do it all again for her.

All I want to do now is to put my arms around her and hold on to her until we become old and decrepit and even after we are dead I want us to be buried in the same grave. Our flesh disintegrating, our bones entwined.

CHAPTER FIFTY

Liliana

I touch my father's hand. "How did you find me so fast?"

"Fast? Hell, Liliana, do you know what one and a half weeks of hell feels like?"

"I'm so sorry, Dad. I never meant to hurt you. I thought I came up with a believable story. I thought I could protect Mum."

"Believable?" He snorts.

"Don't make me laugh. It hurts when I laugh."

His cellphone rings. He looks at it and smiles. "Your mother just touched down in France. Shane and Dom are with her and they'll be here in half an hour."

I smile back. "Good. How did Mum take it?"

He frowns. "Terribly. I was scared for her."

"I'm sorry."

"It's okay. It's not your fault. Everything will be all right now that we've found you."

"How did you find me?"

"When it comes to the underworld no one has better connections than I do. One of Brand's men boasted about the kidnap to a prostitute. She wanted the reward and I wanted the information."

"Dad, why was my story not believable? You did go behind my back and get me that internship and I had every right to be angry and go off on a sulking trip to Spain."

"You called me Daddy. You haven't called me Daddy since you were five years old, honey."

"Oh." I bite my bottom lip. "Dad?"

"Yes."

"Do you think you'll be able to forgive Brand one day? Maybe?"

He keeps his face expressionless. "Maybe. One day."

"He's been through a terrible time, Dad. They did unimaginably horrible things to him after he left our house." I start to sob.

My Dad strokes my head gently. "Hey, stop that. I will forgive him one day, but it will take time. He kidnapped my baby. If anything had happened to you ..." He stops, takes a deep breath, and forces a smile. "Believe me, if he had been anybody else I would have torn his fucking throat out."

"I really love him, Dad."

"Are you sure? Don't rush into anything. You have been through an ordeal. You think you're in love with your captor, but things might look different in time. You just need a bit of time to heal."

I reach up and touch my father's face. "Dad. You know how you feel about, Mum? Do you think you will ever change your mind?"

"It's different."

"No, it's not. Remember when you told me you don't choose love it chooses you. That's exactly what happened to both of us. All these years I was waiting for him and he was waiting for me. We are perfect together. You'll see."

CHAPTER FIFTY-ONE

Brand

I come into the room and her whole face lights up in a bright smile, but I feel sick to my stomach. She looks so damn pale. She lifts her arm in a beckoning gesture. I walk up to the side of the bed.

"I'm so sorry, Liliana. Somehow I managed to get you hurt again."

"Don't be silly. It had nothing to do with you. It all started when a boy called Pierre told me the best way to a man's heart is to get helpless. He suggested breaking an arm or a leg. So of course, I thought I'd go one better and get myself shot in the stomach."

I try to smile, but I can't.

"Come on, Brand."

"That Pierre should mind his own damn business and watch his mouth while he's at it. Giving crap advice to other men's girlfriends."

Her eyes widen. "Oh, my goodness. You just called me your

girlfriend. I think I like that very much."

"Think you like that better than wife?"

Her eyes nearly pop out of their sockets. "What? You're going to make an honest woman out of me, Brand Vaughan."

I shuffle my feet. "Yeah, I'm going to make an honest woman out of you, Liliana Eden."

She grins. "You're going to get an engagement ring for me and everything?"

"Um …I got one already."

She raises her eyebrows. "Really? When did you do that?"

"I bought it seven years ago. I was passing a shop and I saw this ring and it was the exact same color as your eyes so I bought it and kept it. I told myself I was just doing it because it was beautiful, but I guess my heart always knew."

She entwines her fingers with mine. "You know, I'm almost afraid this is a dream and I'll wake up."

"This is no dream, Princess."

"Then I swear I am the luckiest person alive."

"Nah, you're going to have to fight me for that title. Because nobody is luckier than me. I got the woman of my dreams."

She looks up at me saucily. "Yes, I have to agree with you. You are very, very lucky to have me. I'm a bit of a catch, aren't I?"

"Yes, you are. Hey, I wanted to ask you something. What was that reference you made to the story of the Monk and the prostitute?"

She pats the space next to her. "Come on. Make yourself

comfortable. It's a good story. I have to warn you though that in this story you are playing the part of the prostitute."

I gingerly perch next to her and she begins her story.

"In ancient India, monks were not allowed to hang around in any area for too long. The reason for this being that they lived by begging for food and didn't want to become a burden on the poor villagers. The only time they would double down in one area was during the monsoon season which lasted for about three months. At that time the mountain passes were impossible to cross so they had no choice but to stay with one household.

"Before the season started all the monks would go to the head monk's hut and tell him who they were planning to stay with. That was when one of the monks announced he had been invited to stay with the local prostitute.

"All the other monks were suitably scandalized. How can a monk stay with a prostitute in a one room house? She would be a bad influence on him. There would be too many temptations in his path. Her ways were godless. Even the head monk wondered if it was a good idea.

"But the monk who had been invited remained calm. He said he didn't see what the fuss was all about. He was a monk because he believed his way was the best way to live in this world, but if the prostitute's way was better then there was no reason for him to be a monk. In the end the head monk agreed to let him stay with the prostitute.

"For three months the monk lived with the prostitute. During this time she plied her trade. Men came. She danced. There was music and alcohol and fine food served. All the other monks were worried about the state of the monk.

"Once the three months were up, the monk went to see the head monk and with him he had a new recruit. The prostitute had decided to become a monk."

"Your father told you this story?"

"Mmm..."

I nod. "It's a good story."

"You're only a criminal because you don't know a better way, Brand. There is a better way for us and we'll find it together."

I look at her in awe. At this amazing woman who agreed to be mine. Something hurts inside me. "I'm sorry I was such asshole to you. I'm so ashamed of the way I tried to humiliate and debase you."

"Hey, don't be ashamed of the intensity of your passion. You are the boy who loved the rose so much he never let go even when its thorns grew out of his flesh."

"Now...what does a woman have to do around here to get kissed?"

I bend my head and kiss her. She smells of medicine and chemicals, but the magic is still all there and it makes me burn with desire. "I love you," I whisper into her sweet mouth.

"I love you much, much more," she says, tightening her grip on my hand. "Even right now as I speak to you ... my heart feels like it's melting. Even my feet, they feel like they're not really on the mattress. It's like I'm floating ... in this ... in this bubble of ridiculously delicious heat and joy and ... magic."

"You know this is forever. I'll never let you go," I say.

"Forever and ever," she whispers back.

EPILOGUE

Jake

Three years later

https://www.youtube.com/watch?v=xMtuVP8Mj4o

stand at the window and look out at snow. It's what everybody wanted. A white Christmas. In the glass I can see the reflection of my family. Everyone is here. My mother, my siblings and their families, my wife, my children, Brand, Lindy, and my first grandchild. There is something special about him.

From the first moment I saw him in the hospital I knew he was destined for great things. They named him Hunter. He's two years old now and, he has the gift of the gab. I mean, Liliana was a handful, but this little fellow. He takes the cake.

"Remember our first Christmas together?" my wife asks next to me.

I drain my glass and turn to watch her profile. Yes, I remember. Just like I remember every Christmas since then. "What? When you took off all your clothes and enticed me into the hot tub?"

"Hmm … that's not how I remember it. Didn't you take off all my clothes and we never made it to the hot tub?"

Yeah, that is always how it is when I am with her. Before I can answer, Liliana comes running up to us. "Uncle Shane and Uncle Dom are going to set off the fireworks. You guys coming or what?"

"Yeah, we're coming," my wife says.

"You go on first. I'll be along in a minute. I just want to get a refill." I lift my glass to show her it is empty.

As I walk to the bar I see Brand getting his son into his jacket. I stop to watch. Once I was doing that. How fast the time has gone. My children are all adults now. Sometimes I wish I could go back to those innocent days. Brand zips Hunter in and stands. He has no idea how he will miss these days. Even if I told him he wouldn't understand. You only realize how precious it is when it is gone. The boy runs off at the speed of a trapped rat.

Brand glances in my direction and smiles at me. I nod at him. I kept him at a distance for a long time because I wanted to make sure he did right by Liliana. She was so young when she made her choice of a mate, but they are perfect for each other. He's a good lad. He just had an unlucky start. I'm glad he's under my protection now.

He starts walking towards me. Sometimes when I see Brand I see a little of me in him. A gypsy through and through. Loyal and fiercely protective of those he loves. The way it should be. I put out two glasses on the counter and start pouring the whisky. As he approaches me I hand him the glass.

"Merry Christmas, Brand."

"Merry Christmas to you too, Jake."

We knock our drinks back. "Sometimes I think of that night. Do you think you would have pulled the trigger if Liliana had not come into the room? I know I wouldn't have. I was too much in awe of you."

Yes, I would have shot him in the heart no question, but there's no need for me to tell him anything, he'll understand when he has a daughter. "Well, we'll never know the answer to that one, will we? But it all worked out fine. Liliana got to keep her father and gained a husband."

He nods. "I'm glad you didn't too."

Outside the fireworks have already started. The sky is filled with orange sparks. I can hear Hunter screaming his head off. Life is good. Damn good.

That's all folks!

Curious about Jake Eden?
:-)
Read his story
HERE

COMING NEXT...

CAN'T LET HER GO

Chapter 1
Katya

The old church is completely deserted. I huddle into my coat in the freezing air and slip into my usual middle pew. The wood is so cold it seeps right through my clothes and chills my skin. I try to close my eyes and pray, but it is impossible. My mind is full of a thousand whirling things.

"Hello, Katya."

Recognizing the voice, I snap my eyes open, and get to my feet. "Good morning, Father."

The priest beams happily at me. "How are you, child? You will be leaving soon for America, won't you?"

"In three days."

He nods, his cheeks rosy with wine. "You must be very proud of yourself. It is a great opportunity for you and a wonderful thing for your parents, not to mention for our village, and this blessed Church."

I bow my head respectfully. "Yes, Father."

He fingers the cross at the end of his rosary chain. "Well, tell your parents I might pop in tomorrow at teatime. I have a special treat for them. They deserve it. They are giving up their eldest daughter for the good of our community."

I smile politely. "Yes, Father."

"You won't forget us when you are in the land of milk and honey, will you?" he teases, a twinkle in his eye.

"Of course not," I say solemnly.

"Good," his face becomes suddenly grave, "because your parents will be very sad if you do."

"I'll write back all the time and send money when I can."

He nods and looks pleased. "Good girl. I know you'll make us all proud." He takes a deep breath. "Right. I better be off. I need to prepare for my morning sermon tomorrow. Continue with your prayers, child, and I'll see you at your parent's house." He raises a playful eyebrow and waggles his index finger as if I'm going to turn eight and not eighteen in three days. "You never know there might be a little gift for you too."

"Thank you, Father."

The sound of his hard, black shoes echo in the silent church as I sit down and bow my head. The sound stops when he passes into the inner chambers.

I bow my head and make another attempt at prayer. Of course, it is a great honor and a wonderful opportunity for me. I have been told many times that I should be grateful I am good-looking enough to have been chosen to represent my village. Once I have done my duty I will be offered a well-paying job. To that end, I have been taught to speak English from the time I was entered into this program.

But I can't help thinking that in three days, on Delivery day or D-day, I will be sent off to America as if I'm no more than high-end, carefully cultivated livestock. Like one of those Japanese black cows that become Kobe beef. No one will say it out loud, but that is exactly what I am. Raised to fulfill a rich man's desire.

It's been like that for almost forty years in my village. A girl on her eighteenth birthday is given away every five years. During other years, girls from other villages fill in the gap. I'll be the eighth girl from Sutgot.

When I was twelve years old my parents sent pictures of me and to their delight I was accepted into the program. Since then they have been getting a monthly stipend which is supposed to continue for the next ten years and from that day onwards, not a day has passed when they've not reminded me of my obligation to remain pure and unsullied. My entire value is based on that.

I tell myself I should be happy because I am helping my parents. If not for me it would be very hard for them. They are hoping to move away from Sutgot. They want to go to the coast where it's warmer. My father is already thinking of sending my sister's photo when she turns twelve.

There is a shuffling sound behind me and I look around to see someone else has entered the church. Mrs. Komarov nods at me and goes to light a candle. She is wearing the standard kerchief around her head, but hers is silk. I suppose she can afford it since it was her daughter who had her D-day five years ago.

I shut my eyes and give pray one last chance, but my mind simply isn't here. I don't think God is listening to my prayers, anyway. If He were, there would be no delivery day for me. Eventually, I slip out of my pew and head for the exit.

To my surprise, I find Mrs. Komarov waiting just inside the exit. She looks anxious and frightened. "Katya," she begins, a tremor in her voice, "I feel I need to warn you."

I feel the hairs at the back of my neck rise. "Warn me?"

"Five years ago, it was my Saskia that went away. She was a good girl, a very good girl. In all the five years, I've never once heard from her. She was not that kind of girl. She would not forget her family. She would let us know she's alive. We raised her better than that."

I swallow the fear. "Do you mean to say you don't know what happened to her?"

"I spoke to the parents of the girls from the other villages and they have *all* never heard from their daughters once they go even though they are all not bad girls who would never forget their mothers." She glances around nervously. "You must be careful. You must be on guard. The truth is no one knows what really happens to our girls once they leave Sutgot."

Mrs. Komarov glances over her shoulder as if someone might be listening. She grabs my hand and squeezes hard. "You must not forget your mother and your father. You must let them know you're all right. And if you meet my Saskia, you must tell your parents, so they can tell me. Please, please, please, promise me, you will do this."

She's is so desperate and half-crazy with fear I can't help

pitying her. "I promise," I tell her. "I promise to let my parents know. And if I find Saskia, I'll make sure you find out."

There are tears in her eyes, and she opens her mouth, but can't find any words to say. Suddenly she pulls me close and kisses my forehead. She smells of lavender powder. Her body is trembling and I get the feeling she thinks she's sending me to my death. In her mind D-day isn't Delivery-day, it's Death-day.

Then she crosses herself and hurries out the door.

I stand frozen to the spot staring at her. If all those parents didn't hear from their daughters, that means...that means...it's not all sugar and happiness on the other side. I knew Mrs. Komarov's daughter. A good girl. Why in the world wouldn't she write to her mother? It didn't make any sense at all.

My knees are shaking as I walk home. I dare not even...I should talk to my parents. That is what I should do, but they have already had the money from the program, and they are expecting more.

Oh dear God...what is going to happen to me?

Preorder at Amazon:
Can't Let Her Go

ALSO BY GEORGIA

Owned

42 Days

Besotted

Seduce Me

Love's Sacrifice

Masquerade

Pretty Wicked (novella)

Disfigured Love

Hypnotized

Crystal Jake 1,2&3

Sexy Beast

Wounded Beast

Beautiful Beast

Dirty Aristocrat

You Don't Own Me 1 & 2

You Don't Know Me

Blind Reader Wanted

Redemption

The Heir

Blackmailed By The Beast

Submitting To The Billionaire
The Bad Boy Wants Me
Nanny & The Beast
His Frozen Heart
The Man In The Mirror

13616634R00162

Printed in Germany
by Amazon Distribution
GmbH, Leipzig